"How about a d...
good to be hidin...

A dance.

With Chase Mackey.

That took Hadley by surprise.

"Really?" she said before she knew she was going to, the question coming from days long gone by when she'd been alone in her room at home, knowing a school dance was going on without her, only imagining herself there with Chase, dancing...

"Sure, why not?" he answered as if it were nothing—which, to him, she knew was the case.

Then he stood and pulled her chair out for her.

In her fantasies he would take her by the hand and lead her onto the dance floor.

In reality he just barely touched the back of her arm to urge her in that direction.

But it was enough to give her goose bumps that she hoped he didn't notice.

And then they reached the dance floor.

And there she was, dancing with Chase Mackey....

Dear Reader,

Young fantasies and crushes—I had them and so did Hadley McKendrick. Hadley had it rough growing up overweight. But she'd found solace in the crush she'd had on her older brother's best friend, Chase Mackey.

Of course, that was long ago and is now behind her. She's turned her life around, lived in Europe and has come back home to Northbridge to begin a new phase.

Part of that new phase just happens to include working with and living very near Chase Mackey. But Hadley isn't worried about it. The crush is over. Chase is still her brother's best friend and now also his business partner, and there is no way Hadley will let anything develop between her and Chase to put so much for her brother in jeopardy.

Except that what inspired that old crush in the first place has only improved with time. Chase himself has only improved with time. And if Hadley had thought he was irresistible years ago, it's nothing compared to the current Chase.

Welcome home to Northbridge!

Victoria Pade

THE BACHELOR, THE BABY AND THE BEAUTY

VICTORIA PADE

SPECIAL EDITION

Published by Silhouette Books

America's Publisher of Contemporary Romance

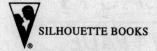

SILHOUETTE BOOKS

ISBN-13: 978-0-373-65544-1

Recycling programs
for this product may
not exist in your area.

THE BACHELOR, THE BABY AND THE BEAUTY

Books by Victoria Pade

VICTORIA PADE

is a _USA TODAY_ bestselling author of numerous romance novels. She has two beautiful and talented daughters—Cori and Erin—and is a native of Colorado, where she lives and writes. A devoted chocolate lover, she's in search of the perfect chocolate chip cookie recipe. For information about her latest and upcoming releases, and to find recipes for some of the decadent desserts her characters enjoy, log on to www.vikkipade.com.

Chapter One

"He'll be right here. He was on his way into town when the moving truck he was driving broke down. My brother went to get him," Hadley McKendrick explained.

Hadley didn't have a clue as to why Neily Pratt-Grayson had dropped in on this September Saturday morning looking for Chase Mackey, her brother Logan's best friend and business partner. And the social worker wasn't giving anything away.

Instead she said, "I'm sorry to show up now, with the wedding tomorrow and all."

Definitely *and all,* Hadley thought as her stomach churned in anticipation of Chase's return to Northbridge, Montana.

Neily was talking about Logan's wedding tomorrow. But to Hadley *and all* meant more than the wedding. Because on top of that, not only would Chase Mackey's arrival be the first time he'd set eyes on her since they were teenagers and Hadley had been a hundred pounds heavier, to Hadley there was also a little matter of an old crush she'd secretly had on Chase.

"Chase isn't only coming for the wedding now, right?" Neily said then. "He's coming for good, isn't he?"

Hadley's stomach took another turn. "This is it," she confirmed. "He'll be here to stay from today on. His place is a huge loft in the top half of the old barn, above what we're using as the workroom and the showroom."

For Mackey and McKendrick Furniture Designs— the business that Logan and Chase owned together, the business that Hadley was now working for. With her brother and Chase…

She just could not stay still another minute!

"Are you sure I can't get you a cup of coffee or a soda or even a glass of water?" Hadley asked hospitably, hoping desperately for the chance to get up from where she was sitting in the living room with Neily and do something to work off a little of the nervous energy that was making her edgy.

"No, thanks, I'm fine," Neily said. "I'm actually here on business or I really wouldn't be bothering you today."

It had been obvious that this wasn't a social call, but Hadley had no idea what business the Northbridge social worker could have with Chase Mackey. He hadn't lived here in over seventeen years. And even when he and Logan had decided to move back, to relocate Mackey and McKendrick Furniture Designs this past spring, Chase had stayed in New York to deal with that end of the move while Logan had handled this end. According to Logan, Chase had been in town only a few times before Hadley had come back to Northbridge in June, and he hadn't been there even once since then.

But he was on his way now and Hadley really couldn't keep herself contained for a minute longer.

"I need just a quick run to the bathroom," she announced to Neily, nearly leaping to her feet.

"Go ahead," Neily encouraged. "Don't worry about me."

Hadley made a beeline for the downstairs bathroom in her brother's house for no reason other than to check on her appearance.

Of course she'd taken extra-special pains with it today, knowing that Chase was coming. She was wearing her tightest jeans and a body-hugging camisole that outlined every inch of her reduced body. After years in the fashion industry, she'd picked up more than one hair and makeup trick and she'd used them all today. Her smoky green eyes were accentuated to their best effect and the high cheekbones that had emerged from beneath the extra weight were highlighted. Not a single pore marred her skin. Her mauve lipgloss looked perfectly natural and her russet-brown, chin-length hair glistened as it fell around her face and showed off her new highlights.

No one who remembered her from her youth in Northbridge hadn't dropped a jaw when they'd seen the transformation in her. She'd taken it in stride—she'd lost the weight so long ago that, to her, it had stopped being the most monumental part of her life. But knowing that this would be the first time Chase Mackey would see her this way? Okay, yes, she wanted his jaw to drop.

It was just human nature to want the object of an old crush to notice a thing like that. It didn't mean that the old crush was still in effect in any way, she assured herself.

The muted sound of a car coming nearer on the road that led to the house alerted Hadley. There were only two possibilities for who it could be: Logan's fiancée Meg, with his three-year-old daughter, Tia, or Logan bringing Chase back from the stalled moving truck.

It was that second possibility that gave Hadley jitters and made her feel as if she was sixteen again.

But she wasn't sixteen, she lectured herself. She was thirty-three. She'd been married. Divorced. She'd lived in Europe for the past ten years. It was ridiculous to be nervous about seeing someone who, ultimately, had only been a fringe part of her youth.

Even if she'd used that fringe part to fuel fantasies

galore and an adoration that most teenage girls had reserved for rock stars.

But that was ancient history. She and Logan and Chase were going to work together and live in close proximity. She was going to behave the same way she would with anyone else who might be a friend of her brother's and a business associate of them both. Friendly. Professional. Detached.

So there was no cause for her to be nervous or jittery or uncomfortable. Logan had said that Chase had never given any indication that he had the slightest clue as to how she'd felt about him. Which meant that she didn't have to worry.

Hadley took a deep, cleansing breath, feeling better. It shouldn't be so hard to face him. It should be fine.

Then she heard the sound of deep male voices coming in the back door and she knew it wasn't Meg and Tia who were home. It was Logan and Chase.

"He never knew," she whispered to herself to bolster her courage. "He doesn't ever need to know."

Another deep breath—this one to give her strength—and Hadley opened the bathroom door, stepping out into the hallway just as Chase Mackey appeared at the other end near the kitchen.

His sharply-edged jaw didn't drop when he saw her. But his eyebrows arched over sky-blue eyes that were more remarkable than she remembered.

"Had-Had-Hadley? Is that you?" he asked in enough shock and awe to please her, using the silly version of her name that he'd made up when they were kids. That only he had ever used.

"It's me," she confirmed, wondering how it was possible for him to have gotten even better looking.

But he had.

Not that he was picture-perfect the way the male models she'd worked with were. Chase had a less refined, rugged, masculine handsomeness built around those eyes. His nose was slightly long, his lower lip was fuller than his upper, and his forehead was probably wider than a photographer would have wanted.

But he also had wavy, golden-brown hair cut short on the sides and left just a touch longer on top. There was a slight crease in the very center of his chin that added to his appeal. Over six feet tall, he had a lean, muscular body lurking behind his jeans and T-shirt. There was no denying that Chase Mackey was still a jaw-dropper himself.

"You look amazing," he exclaimed—saying to her what she was thinking about him. "I don't think I would have known you if we'd met on the street."

"I'm half the woman I was," Hadley joked.

"It's more than the weight—"

But years of carrying the weight had caused her to be very self-conscious, and while she was thrilled with his reaction, she couldn't be comfortable under his scrutiny for long. And Neily was a built-in way out. So before he could go on with what he was about to say, Hadley interrupted him.

"We can catch up later. I don't know if you remember Neily Pratt or not, but she's waiting in the living room to see you."

"Neily is here?" Logan said, stepping up behind Chase just then.

"I remember the Pratt family," Chase said, "but not specifically Neily...."

"She needs to see you," Hadley repeated.

"Hi," Neily said, suddenly appearing from the living room to join them.

Logan greeted Neily warmly and after some further back-and-forth that helped Chase place who she was, she said, "I apologize for being here the minute you walk in the door, Chase, and on the day before your wedding, Logan, but I'm afraid I'm here on business that couldn't wait."

"Furniture business?" Logan asked.

"Social-worker business. With Chase."

Chase and Logan looked as confused by that as Hadley was.

"Maybe you and Chase should talk alone," Hadley suggested out of courtesy, despite her own curiosity.

"That's okay," Chase said. "I can't imagine what business I could have with a social worker, but I'm probably gonna end up talking about it with you after the fact anyway, so we might as well skip a step."

Neily pointed over her shoulder in the direction from which she'd just come. "I have a file…"

"Let's all go in the living room, then," Logan suggested.

They did, with Neily returning to her spot on the sofa and Hadley taking the easy chair again while Chase and Logan remained standing, facing them.

"I don't know how much of your background you know, Chase," Neily began.

"I was orphaned at three when my folks were killed in a car accident—about six months after we moved to Northbridge," Chase supplied.

"And did you know that you had siblings?"

That was not anything Hadley had ever heard, and from the look on Chase's face, it was news to him, too.

"There was just me," he claimed.

"Actually, there was also an older half sister, a younger sister and two younger brothers—twins," Neily said, opening the file that she'd taken onto her lap.

Chase focused on Logan. "Is this a welcome-home prank?"

Logan seemed dumbfounded himself as he shook his head. "Like I don't have enough going on with the wedding?"

"It isn't a prank," Neily assured them.

"I don't remember any brothers or sisters," Chase said.

"According to the file, you were barely three—in fact you were a month short," Neily said patiently. "We don't actually begin to retain memory until about four unless it's something traumatic. But by the same token, a traumatic event—like losing your family, being taken out of your home—could wipe out some memories, too. What *do* you recall?"

"My earliest memory is of the boys' home. There were some dreams... But that's all they were—dreams."

"If they involved sisters and brothers, they weren't just dreams. They must have been your brain's way of reminding you. What about your parents—do you remember them?"

Chase shook his head. "Not really. I have an old wedding picture of them that I've stared at enough to know their faces and I think that's sort of *become* my memory of them. But to say that I actually remember anything about them—the way they looked other than that picture, or the sound of their voices or ever being with them? No, I don't. Still, it seems like if I'd ever had brothers and sisters I would have remembered *that*," he said.

"But you don't," Neily concluded. "And you *do* have them. Your older sister—her name was Angie Cragen—"

"Was?" Logan interjected.

"Was," Neily confirmed. "She was actually your half sister, Chase. Your mother had her when she was seventeen and never married her father. But Angie Cragen was born with a congenital heart problem and she died last week."

Hadley could see that this was one shock piled on

another for Chase and to allow him a moment, she said, "How do you know this stuff, Neily?"

"There's a lawyer in Billings who's involved and now so is Human Services there—a social worker contacted me and I've spoken to the lawyer, too. Knowing she didn't have long to live, Angie Cragen hired the lawyer before her death. Since Angie was eight when the accident happened, she remembered you, Chase, and the other kids. After the accident, because she had a birth father, she went to live with him while the rest of you went into foster care."

Hadley wasn't sure if it was the mention of foster care or something else that brought a dark frown to Chase's handsome face.

"The other three kids were adopted," Neily continued. "But because you weren't, Chase, you retained the Mackey name and that's why your half sister was able to locate you."

"It's a little late, isn't it?"

"I only know what I was told, and according to the lawyer, once Angie Cragen began to search for her siblings, it took until just before her death to track you down. She would have liked to contact you herself but she was getting sicker and sicker and—"

"Hold on," Chase said.

His hands went to his narrow hips as he switched his weight from one foot to the other. It took Hadley a moment to realize she was looking at those hips. Appreciating the sight.

She yanked her eyes upward and forced herself to concentrate on what he was saying.

"Some sick and dying woman who hadn't put the effort into looking me up for thirty-two years decided to do it now? Why?"

"There's a child," Neily said quietly. "Angie Cragen had an eleven-month-old son and no one to raise him after her death. I'm not sure of the details. She made a recording that I've been told explains the whole thing; it's here in the file." Neily patted the folder she had on her lap. "But what I do know is that she wanted her son to go one of her half siblings because you are the only family she had left. She wanted him raised by a blood relation. And since you're the only one of the siblings she managed to locate—"

"A stranger left me her kid?" Chase said. "Now I know this has to be some kind of joke."

"It's no joke," Neily said. "Your half sister hoped that even though she didn't have the chance to meet you or speak to you, you would still step up and raise your nephew. Or at least take him while you go on to find your other sister and brothers to see if one of them might want him…."

Chase glanced at Logan, again. "Tell me now if this is some hoax."

With an expression as perplexed as Chase's, Logan shrugged, shook his head and said, "Honest to God, Chase, I don't have anything to do with this."

Frowning deeply, Chase looked back to Neily but

before he said anything else, she said, "I know this is a shock and I want to make it clear that you are in no way obligated to take this child. When Angie died, Human Services stepped in and he's been placed in foster care—"

"The kid is in foster care?" Chase demanded as if that was a bigger deal than Neily had made it sound.

"He's with a foster family in Billings. But they can't keep him more than a few days because they're already overloaded—that's why I'm here now. Before finding him another home, the lawyer insisted that you be presented with all of this so that—if you were willing to take the baby the way Angie Cragen hoped you would— he could come here rather than be handed off to another temporary placement."

Chase closed his eyes and once more shook his head in what looked to be utter disbelief.

Then he opened them, scowled at Neily and said, "You're sure this kid is related to me? You're absolutely, without-a-doubt positive?"

"Everything tracks," Neily confirmed. "But again, Chase, you're under no obligation—"

"I'll take him. For now," Chase said, abruptly cutting off more of Neily's words.

Chase Mackey, player of all time—according to what Logan had said about him over the years—wasn't hesitating to take on an eleven-month-old baby out of the blue?

That surprised Hadley more than the way she looked had surprised Chase when he'd first seen her.

"A baby is a lot of work and responsibility," Neily warned as if she wasn't altogether comfortable with his hasty decision. "We're talking about an *infant*—diapers, bottles, nighttime feedings... Do you have any experience at all with—"

"Doesn't matter," Chase decreed. "Logan did that stuff with Tia—if he could do it, I can do it. He can show me how. If the kid is related to me, I won't see him get sucked any further into the system than he already has been."

There was decisiveness and determination behind his words that Hadley didn't quite understand. But she assumed it had something to do with the fact that Chase had avoided his own foster home in favor of spending a lot of time at the McKendrick house.

"I'm not saying I'll keep him," Chase went on as if he didn't want Neily to believe he was making more of a commitment than he was. "I'm just saying that I'll take him and go on looking for... What was it? Another sister and two brothers? Then if one of them is better suited to raise the kid, I'll probably turn him over to them. But for now..." Chase suddenly switched his focus to Logan again and spoke to him, "I'm gonna need some help..."

"Sure. Whatever. You know that," Logan assured.

Chase glanced back at Neily. "Then, yeah, I guess you can bring it on."

Hadley thought Neily seemed uneasy with this. Then she confirmed it by saying, "If you change your mind either before the baby gets here—"

"Which will be when? Do you have him out in your car or something?" Chase asked.

Neily flinched slightly at that notion.

"The baby is in Billings. It will be Monday before I'll be able to make the transfer. But if you change your mind before then or at any time after that, you just have to call me and I'll come for him."

"And stick him back in a foster home," Chase muttered under his breath. But to Neily he said, "I'll keep that in mind." Then, obviously thinking ahead, he said, "These other people—are they all Angie Cragen's half brothers and half sister, but my full siblings?"

"They are your full brothers and sister, yes."

"And do you know if the half sister was at least close to finding any of them?"

"I don't know that, no. I only know that you are the only one the lawyer could actually give us enough information about to make contact." Neily held up the file. "There's the DVD—it might have more information on the others. And there's a picture of the baby here among the paperwork if you'd like to see him. I'll leave it all for you."

Hadley saw Neily's hesitation when she stood to hand the file to Chase.

"Does he have a name?" Chase asked then, not opening the file to even glance at the baby's picture the way Hadley would have.

"Cody. The baby's name is Cody," Neily informed him.

"Cody," Chase repeated.

"Well, if you're sure…" Neily said, pausing to offer Chase a second chance to say no.

When he didn't, she said, "If you're sure, I'll go and make the arrangements now, and then I'll see you all tomorrow at the wedding and again on Monday with the baby."

Chase merely nodded as Hadley stood up to walk Neily out.

It wasn't until the front door was closed behind the social worker and Hadley had turned back to the two men that she heard Chase mutter to Logan, "What the hell just happened? I have family?"

"Including an eleven-month-old nephew who you just agreed to take on…" Logan said with some disbelief of his own.

"Oh, man, I did, didn't I?" Chase said as if it were just sinking in.

"Come on, let's get your stuff out to the loft," Logan suggested. "Then maybe you can watch that DVD."

Chase nodded, still looking stunned. He headed for the kitchen, catching sight of Hadley as he did and coming up short all over again.

"Wow, and you, Hadley… You've blown me away, too."

Hadley laughed. "It's still just me. With a little less packaging."

"Yeah, I can see that it's still you," he assured. "But that's good, too—it's good to see…you," he added.

Hadley merely smiled at him, at his confusion over her transformation. But she was pleased that he recognized that not everything about her had changed.

"Later, I guess," he added with a sigh as he again aimed for the kitchen.

"Sure. I'll see you later," she confirmed, watching him go and trying not to register that his backside was almost as impressive as his front.

Then her brother distracted her by whispering as he went by, "I'm gonna need your help big-time!"

Hadley wasn't quite sure what her brother was going to need her help with, but that wasn't uppermost in her mind.

Chase was.

Chase and the news that had just been sprung on him and his instant agreement to accept the responsibility of his half nephew.

But then Hadley heard the back door open and close and it struck her just like that—her first encounter with Chase Mackey in seventeen years was over…

She'd successfully jumped that hurdle.

And she breathed a sigh of relief.

Granted, their reunion had taken a backseat to Neily's news, but still, Hadley thought she'd done okay before that. No, she hadn't been smooth or glib or clever—the way she'd imagined herself in one of the many scenarios she'd played out in anticipation of this—but she hadn't embarrassed herself, either. She was relatively sure she'd hidden her tension, that she'd appeared reasonably normal.

And the first hurdle was the highest, she told herself. From here on every time she saw Chase it would get easier. She would feel less awkward, she would be able to relax more. Eventually she would forget all about that crush she'd had on him so many years ago and forge a plain and simple working relationship with him.

And that was all she was looking forward to, she told herself.

Even if the image of those blue eyes of his was mysteriously lingering in her mind and making it seem as if she might be looking forward to something more than that...

Chapter Two

"You want me to stick around?"

Chase couldn't help smiling at his friend's offer. He knew Logan was swamped with last-minute wedding details.

"Do you think I need a babysitter?"

"That *is* one of the things you'll need after Monday," Logan goaded wryly.

"Or maybe a pretty little nanny…" Chase volleyed good-naturedly, referring to the fact that Logan was about to marry his daughter's caregiver.

"Knowing you, I'm sure you'll run through plenty of those," Logan countered with a laugh.

All kidding aside, Chase let his friend off the hook. "It's weird to find out I might have brothers and a sister, and that in a day and a half I'll be taking on a kid who's supposed to be my nephew. But the earth hasn't stopped turning because of any of it. Get going on that honey-do list you told me you have in your pocket. I'm fine."

"You're sure?"

"Yeah, go on."

It didn't take more than that for Logan to head for the door. "Meg stocked a few groceries in your fridge, but for anything other than snacking you can hit ours. Come over whenever you're ready,"

"Thanks," Chase said to his partner's back as Logan left him alone in the loft Chase had designed and Logan had built.

With all Chase had had to do back in New York, he hadn't made it to Northbridge since late May. At that point the space he'd taken for himself in the top half of what had formerly been a barn had been in the final stages of construction.

A quick glance around at the large, open area and Chase knew that Logan had made sure the contractor met his specifications.

His furniture had been sent ahead last week. He'd trusted his own belongings to professional movers while he'd manned the truck—that was now stalled just outside of town—filled with the Mackey and McKendrick Designs pieces that were slated for the Northbridge showroom. The movers had set his things around the place haphazardly—the furniture was usable but still needed to be arranged the way he wanted it.

But Chase had more important things on his mind. Despite what he'd led his friend to think, he was a little shaken to suddenly find out he hadn't been an only child.

How the hell could he have blanked on something like brothers and sisters? he asked himself as he went to the chrome-and-glass kitchen table and tossed the social worker's file folder onto it.

Okay, yes, he had been barely more than a baby when his parents were killed—six months younger than Tia was now, and she was just a tiny, tiny kid.

And yes, there had been dreams. Disjointed dreams that had never seemed like anything but dreams—that he had a family, that his parents were alive. But he'd always figured it was just wishful thinking. It had never felt real enough to be anything else, or been clear enough to make him believe there had ever actually been other kids, especially when he honestly had no waking memory of them.

But apparently there had been. Older and younger kids…

Trying now to think back as far as he could, Chase still couldn't recall anything that led up to his going to the boys' home where his first memories began—and even those were vague. He just remembered being at the boys' home, being scared and lonely most of the time there.

Nowhere in that could he remember the slightest

indication that there were siblings he'd been separated from.

Not that he recalled ever asking.

He did remember asking about his parents—though he didn't remember exactly when. He only knew that the answer to his question had been, "They're no longer with us..." He'd thought that that meant they'd gone off somewhere and just left him behind for some reason, maybe because he had done something wrong.

The fact that his parents had died hadn't been openly discussed with him until he'd gone from the boys' home to his foster home.

He'd been eight then. When Alma Pritick had taken the time to talk to him about his mother and father, about what had happened to them.

Alma Pritick had been one of the few positive aspects of his childhood.

It had been Alma who had located an old newspaper clipping of his parents' wedding picture for him and framed it. Alma who had finally given him the sense that at one point he had belonged to someone who cared about him.

But nowhere in any of what Alma had said, either, had there been a mention of other kids who had been orphaned alongside him.

He had never had a clue.

But now that he knew it, he had other things to deal with.

Things like an eleven-month-old nephew...

That still didn't seem real.

But with that baby in mind, he sat on one of the director's chairs that went with the table and opened the file.

The DVD and some paperwork were inside. Along with the photograph of the baby.

Cute enough, as kids went, he thought as he studied the picture. Big brown eyes. Chunky cheeks. Some feathery, light-colored hair that stood up on the top of the kid's head like spikes.

"Okay…" he said as if he'd successfully taken the first step on the detour he'd just made into unknown territory.

And a kid was pretty unknown territory for him. The only one he'd ever had contact with was Tia, and that had been more in the role of sort-of uncle. Initially, when Logan's wife had left Logan with their two-month-old daughter, Chase had gone to Connecticut to help out. But his help had actually just been moral support for Logan—it wasn't as if he'd done much hands-on with Tia.

Diaper changes, feedings, baths—those things had been his friend's purview. He'd held Tia a few times, but that was about it. And in the three years since then? A sort-of uncle—that was what Chase's relationship with Tia had consisted of. There definitely hadn't been anything that would have prepared him for taking care of a kid himself, that was for sure.

But when Neily Pratt had said this new kid was in foster care? That had struck a nerve.

No, his experience in foster care hadn't been a horror story. But he did know the good and the not-so-good sides of it.

Alma Pritick had been the good side.

But there had also been Alma's husband, Homer. And while Homer might not have been abusive, he had definitely been on the not-so-good side of foster care. Homer Pritick and the boys' home before him—those were the memories that had spurred Chase to take the kid. Because the bottom line was that if the child was related to him in any way, he didn't want him in that same system.

"So you're gonna be mine," he said as if he were talking to the baby rather than the baby's picture. "At least for a while…"

Then he set down the photograph and picked up the DVD.

The DVD his older sister had made.

Sisters and brothers…

It just didn't seem possible.

It was Logan who had sisters and brothers, not him.

Sisters like Hadley.

Hadley…

"I couldn't believe my eyes, Had-Had-Hadley," he said to himself as set down the DVD, got up and went to unpack his laptop computer so he could play it.

Sure, over the years Logan had told him that Hadley had slimmed down, but he hadn't given it much thought. Hadley was just Hadley: Logan's sister. Logan had told him things about Tessa and Issa and Zeli—Logan's half sisters—and about his half brothers, too. None of it had meant anything to Chase beyond being Logan's news from home.

But wow, seeing Hadley for himself? She hadn't just lost weight, she'd grown up into a knockout.

Her previously bad skin was porcelain-perfect now. He'd never known she had high cheekbones or that what had just looked like dents in bread dough were actually damn adorable dimples in her cheeks. Her hair wasn't stringy anymore; it was bouncy and smooth and silky and begged to be touched. The rest of her face had been so plump that until today, he'd never known what full, sweet lips she had. And even her eyes somehow seemed more remarkable—green but with a sort of topaz glimmer to them.

And the body! No one would ever guess that that firm, curvy little figure could have been whittled out of what she'd been as a girl.

Man, she was a beauty! A country-girl kind of beauty that made him think of Northbridge and clean air and fresh fields of hay, clear blue skies and snowcapped mountains.

A country-girl kind of beauty that—if things were different—he would have gone after with full force.

But even the new Hadley was still the little sister

of his best friend and business partner, he reminded himself as he took the laptop back to the table. That alone was reason enough to keep his hands off of her, but add to it the fact that Hadley had also come back to Northbridge to be their upholsterer, the fact that they'd be working together, too, and there was no clear sailing for him on waters like that.

At least not with his philosophy on relationships. He never mixed the long-term with the short-term. His friendship and partnership with Logan were definitely long-term. Potentially, Hadley working with them could also be long-term. But a personal relationship with Hadley? A personal relationship with any woman was always short-term for him.

Besides, after the fiasco of his last relationship, he needed a breather from the opposite sex.

And topped off with this family and nephew thing, there was no room for romance even if being with Hadley wasn't outside of his own self-set limits.

But damn if Hadley McKendrick hadn't turned herself into someone who was going to make it tough on him to stick to his limits, he thought as he turned on the computer and waited for it to boot up.

He was going to stick to them, though.

When it came to Hadley, he knew without a doubt that he had to adopt a strict look-but-don't-touch policy.

No matter how good she looked.

And damn, did she look good…

* * *

"It's a lot to ask and I wouldn't, except that this is our honeymoon and you know how excited Tia is to go to Disneyland—I just can't cancel."

"I wouldn't want you to," Hadley assured her brother. "And you're right, Chase is going to need help with that baby—"

"Not just help. He's going to need his hand held from beginning to end—babies aren't his thing. He doesn't know the first thing about them."

Hadley certainly didn't want to think about holding Chase Mackey's hand.

"I'm sure he'll be a fast learner," she said, putting her own hope into words.

Logan had come back from Chase's loft and immediately sought out Hadley in the living room of the main house, where she was hemming Tia's flower-girl dress.

She'd been so lost in thinking about Chase and their first meeting that she hadn't given a second thought to what her brother had said about needing her help— big-time. But now that Logan had asked her to stand in for him, to teach his friend how to care for the nephew Chase had agreed to take on, she was playing it cool. She was acting as if Logan's request hadn't surprised her, as if she wasn't thrown by the idea of being Chase Mackey's companion-in-childcare. But she was hardly as unruffled by the idea as she was pretending to be.

Working with Chase, living near him, seeing a lot

of him—those were things she'd known were coming. Things she'd planned for. Things she'd decided she could handle in a purely friendly acquaintance sort of way that would ease them into this new phase in their lives.

But what her brother was asking of her was something else entirely. She wouldn't have the benefit of Logan being around, or Meg or even Tia. She and Chase would be on their own together. Alone. In his loft a lot of the time, putting a nursery together, caring for an infant, with her holding his hand through it all.

And that was a little unnerving for her.

Still she said, "Whether he learns fast or not, you can't miss your honeymoon to do something that I can easily do."

"Are you sure it's no problem?" Logan asked. "At least the vet is going to neuter the dogs and keep them until we get back, so you won't have Max and Harry to take care of, too, but—"

"I'm sure there's no problem. It'll be fine," she assured her brother, hiding her own misgivings.

Maybe not too well, because Logan's expression was doubtful. "So you didn't have any pangs of the old crush when you saw Chase again?"

"I told you I wouldn't and I didn't," she said. Which was basically true. But she also hadn't been able to ignore the fact that time had only improved Chase's appeal.

She wasn't going to confess that to her brother, though,

so she said, "Since we've been back in Northbridge you've met up with a few girls you dated in high school without having any effect, right? So when it comes to Chase, it's no different for me," she reasoned.

"Okay. I'm not sure why I keep worrying about it." Maybe because he had some awareness that to the over-weight, unattractive young girl she'd been, this crush had been more important in its own way than any of his own casual high-school dating.

Maybe because he had an inkling that her daydreams of Chase had gotten her through some very rough times when teasing at school had been downright mean, and at home when she'd had their malicious stepmother to contend with.

But that was all in the very distant past. She honestly felt sure that she'd left her crush behind with the extra hundred pounds she'd carried around then.

"I guess I just wouldn't want you to try to live out some fantasy," Logan said. "You and Chase aren't on the same wavelength when it comes to—"

"I know—Chase is a so-many-women-so-little-time kind of guy. Don't worry, I've gotten the picture from the things you've told me about him over the years. He plays around. He's like Garth—"

The mention of her ex-husband's name brought a frown edged with anger to her brother's face.

"Chase is nothing like Garth," Logan retorted. "Chase doesn't break commitments to women because he doesn't make commitments to women. Because what

Chase is committed to is his belief that that's the best way for him."

Whatever that meant…

"But ultimately he runs through women like other people run through shoes."

"I just think that, for you, relationships are different than what they are for Chase," Logan said. "And I wouldn't want you to get hurt. But for the record, I've never said Chase runs through women."

"There's been a different one every time I've talked to you over the years. That seems to me like running through women. And after Garth, the last thing I would go anywhere near is a man who's commitment-impaired. So I'm telling you, I might have had some illusions about Chase being the perfect guy nearly twenty years ago, but I don't have any now. I guarantee you, I can show him how to change a diaper without fainting from infatuation."

And she thought that was true. No, she didn't especially want to spend concentrated time alone with Chase, and it would certainly have helped if he looked more like a warthog than the heartthrob leading man in a Western movie. But after eleven years in the European fashion industry, she'd learned to take good looks with a grain of salt, and that was what she intended to do with Chase.

"No matter what you say, you know I've been worried about you being around Chase again and this…well, this really makes me worry," her brother fretted.

"That's because you and I haven't had a lot of time with each other since you left Northbridge. You might have missed it, but I'm not the innocent, naive, dreamy-eyed girl I was before," Hadley said patiently. "And what I believe is that trying to make a one-woman man out of Chase Mackey—or any other man who doesn't want to be a one-woman man—is something only a fool would undertake. And I'm nobody's fool."

"Got it—you're all grown up, you're a woman of the world and you can take care of yourself," Logan said.

"Yes," she confirmed. "And it's really not a big deal for me to help Chase. I'm happy to do it until you get back from your honeymoon."

Okay, happy was not exactly true. But she'd still do it.

"I appreciate it," Logan said.

"It's nothing. Now go do what Meg needed you to do today so you can get to the rehearsal on time tonight."

"Yeah, I better. And thanks—I owe you for this."

Hadley waved him away.

All this talk about gratitude suddenly made her realize that to some extent, helping Chase out now would repay the debt she'd had to him since they were kids.

Growing up, Chase had been unfailingly kind to her, and that wasn't something she could say about everyone, especially not about the boys she'd known back then. In fact, that kindness he'd shown her had probably contributed to why she'd had such a crush on him.

And not only had he been kind to her, but there also

had been a time when he'd come to her rescue, when he'd defended her against people who hadn't been so kind.

For that, she owed him.

Besides, so far she'd managed not to act like a silly schoolgirl with a crush in Chase's presence. What harm could come in helping him out next week while Logan was gone?

None, she told herself.

And if she wasn't going to be able to ease into being around Chase again, then maybe taking the plunge—so to speak—was the next best thing. Maybe the more time she spent with him right off the bat, the quicker she'd be able to overlook his attributes, completely conquer feeling awkward around him and just get on with things.

That didn't seem altogether unfeasible, she decided.

And ultimately, it would all be fine.

Chapter Three

Hadley spent the wedding rehearsal and dinner on Saturday night primarily with her half sisters and half brothers helping to wrangle their three-year-old niece, Tia, and blending in with the rest of the bridesmaids. She never ventured too near Chase and he never ventured too near her.

She caught him staring at her more times than she could count, but took that in stride. It wasn't uncommon for people who had known her when she was heavy to stare when they saw her now. It didn't mean anything except that they were getting accustomed to the transformation in her.

Certainly she didn't take Chase's scrutiny as anything more than that. Or at least she didn't allow herself to think that way. Even if he didn't glance away any of the times she caught him. Even if he did smile each and every time with what she might have taken as appreciation.

But as it was, through all of Saturday evening's events, she kept her distance, steadfastly reminding herself that she and Chase were never going to be more than friendly acquaintances. She made it through the entire time with only a distant hello at the beginning, a distant good-night at the end and nothing but the exchange of those looks in between.

Sunday was a day of helping Meg get ready and again managing Tia. The wedding was late in the afternoon at the church, and afterward the reception was held in what ultimately would be the Mackey and McKendrick Furniture Designs showroom when the moving truck—that had been repaired and brought onto the property—was unloaded.

But for Sunday night the large open space was completely aglow with candlelight. The walls were draped in flowing curtains of white satin to reflect the golden glow and to give a softer appearance to the place. Bronze-and-cream-colored roses were everywhere. There was a long buffet table laden with food and the five-layer wedding cake. Frosted in buttercream, it had cascading fondant flowers from the feet of the bride, groom and little girl figurines on top. White linen-clothed tables were set all around a central area that was reserved for dancing to the music of a string quartet.

Since Chase was the best man and Hadley was one of the bridesmaids, they were both seated at the wedding-party table. But several chairs separated them so Hadley could still maintain her distance. Until the dancing began and they were left alone there while everyone else followed the bride and groom onto the floor.

Then, dressed in a black suit that fitted him impeccably and accentuated the width of his shoulders to mouthwatering perfection, Chase got up from his seat and came to sit sideways in the chair beside Hadley's, facing her.

He slung one arm onto the table and the other over the back of her chair—as relaxed as a brother would have been to approach her and certainly showing no signs that his heart was beating double-time the way hers was.

"I have to tell you, Had-Had-Hadley, that I can't keep my eyes off you," he said with a smile that had gained wattage over the years and made her melt just a little inside. Even so, she continued to face the dance floor, only glancing at him for a moment.

"I know—I don't look anything like the person you knew before. I've been hearing it all summer, ever since I got back to Northbridge."

"The person I knew before was just a kid," he reminded. "But you have come into your own—in more ways than one."

"More than just losing the weight?" she asked, because it was always the weight that everyone talked about and she found it curious that Chase didn't seem to be referring to that alone.

"Sure, more than the weight. You're different all the way around—you don't slouch like you wish you were invisible, you look people in the eye when you talk to them, you smile, you speak up, you seem more confident, more sure of yourself. And on the outside you're just…" He shook his head, giving her the once-over yet again before he said, "You're just gorgeous."

Hadley laughed. He hadn't said that the way a man might have said it to pick her up; he said it more matter-of-factly, in a way that didn't make it sound like empty flattery. In a way that made her almost believe it.

But still she couldn't go along with it. "Gorgeous?" she countered, using a tone she would have adopted with Logan if he were exaggerating something. "I've been around gorgeous. I think it might be a little over-the-top to put me in that category."

"The models you worked with in Italy and France— that's the gorgeous you've been around?"

"They make their living being gorgeous," Hadley confirmed.

"That high-fashion stuff? That might be different than what you are, but you still grew up with your own brand of gorgeous," he insisted, his sincerity and straightforwardness making her feel better than all the other compliments she'd previously received put together.

"And how brave can you get?" he went on marveling. "Taking off to live in Europe—"

"I didn't do that alone," she demurred.

"But you did it. That's the kind of thing people think about—dream about—but don't have the courage to actually do."

"I suppose," Hadley conceded. "But life is life—here or there," she pointed out. "There are still ups and downs and things to get through—" Like her divorce...

But she didn't want to talk about that.

"It was definitely fun," she continued. "And I admit that I amazed myself a little when I actually pulled it off, but—"

"If you could lose half your body weight you could do anything?"

Hadley laughed. "I guess that's true."

"All I know," Chase concluded, "is that you've impressed the hell out of me."

"Then my work is done," she joked, making him laugh a throaty laugh that was more sexy than she could stand.

The subject seemed to change naturally when Case said, "So Logan tells me you've signed on to help me out with this baby I'm inheriting tomorrow."

"Unless you think you can do it yourself..." she said, hoping he would say he could.

"Do it myself? Oh, God, no!" he exclaimed. "I'm an idiot when it comes to babies and kids. I went to Connecticut for a while when Logan got divorced—Tia was a baby—but I never did any hands-on. Then Logan and Tia stayed with me in New York just before their move here, and Tia had to talk me through her breakfast one morning when Logan was on the phone with a client."

"Butter on one half of the slice of toast, peanut butter on the other half, then fold it together—don't cut it?"

"See what I mean? Who knew kids were that quirky? And at least Tia could tell me what she wanted. I don't know the first thing about taking care of a baby and I'm guessing that at eleven months he won't be able to tell me himself."

"No, he won't," Hadley confirmed with a small laugh.

"So it was like being thrown a lifeline when Logan said you'd help out." He leaned in close and said, "You do know about taking care of babies, right?"

Obviously he hadn't been too observant during his visits to her house growing up, or he wouldn't have had to ask that question.

Hadley motioned toward the rest of the room where everyone else was. "I have two younger half brothers and three younger half sisters, remember? My stepmother said the only thing I was good for was to help her with them and babysit so she could have a break. I was changing diapers by the time I was five."

"I do remember your stepmother…" he said, making a gloomy, sympathetic face. "But like I said, I can't tell you what a relief it is to know I won't be on my own with this."

"Neily said you could back out at any time," Hadley reminded him. "A child is a huge responsibility. If you've changed your mind, Neily is out there on the dance floor—you could tell her tonight and—"

"No, I can't do that. Not even now that I've thought about it. I couldn't live with myself."

Again Hadley saw how strongly he felt about this and wondered why. But she didn't feel free to ask.

Then he said, "Did Logan twist your arm about helping me? Are you dreading it?"

"No," Hadley was quick to answer because she didn't want him to know how reluctant she was. "Logan didn't twist my arm. I was just thinking of you…"

"You jumped in with both feet yesterday. There's no sin in changing your mind after realizing what you've gotten yourself into."

"Nope, can't do that. But don't feel as if you have to lend a hand if you don't want to—I'll make do, maybe I can hire someone—"

Why did the thought of that suddenly make her feel territorial? Why was she actually chafing at the suggestion of someone else coming in to do what she'd agreed so reluctantly to do herself?

She had no explanation. And no time to dwell on it.

"No, that would be silly. I honestly don't mind," she lied. "It will give me something to do until you guys get business up and running again and there's furniture for me to upholster."

Which was true enough. The summer had passed with Hadley sewing dresses for this wedding and working with Logan on the showroom itself—cleaning and painting and decorating it in sections as if each were a separate room so the furniture could be arranged and displayed within those settings. But until Logan and Chase got back to actually making new pieces, her only job now was to organize her own workspace.

"So you aren't dreading teaching me how to take care of an eleven-month-old?"

Well, she was. But she would have to lie.

"Not at all," she said, watching her brother and new sister-in-law dance with Tia rather than look Chase in the eye.

"I don't think you mean that, but I'm gonna pretend you do because I really need help," he confided.

The music ended and someone Hadley didn't know stepped up to the microphone to make a toast, saving her from having to go overboard to convince Chase that he was wrong when he wasn't.

Then, after everyone had raised a glass of champagne to wish Meg and Logan well, the quartet began to play again.

And Chase was apparently ready to go on to other things because he said, "How about a dance? You look too good to be hiding behind this table."

A dance.

With Chase Mackey.

That took Hadley by surprise.

"Really?" she said before she knew she was going to, the question coming from days long gone by when she'd been alone in her room at home, knowing a school dance was going on without her, only imagining herself there with Chase, dancing…

"Sure, why not?" he answered as if it were nothing—which, to him, she knew was the case.

Then he stood and pulled her chair out for her.

In her fantasies, he would take her by the hand and lead her onto the dance floor.

In reality he just barely touched the back of her arm to urge her in that direction.

But it was enough to give her goose bumps that she hoped he didn't notice.

And then they reached the dance floor.

He stepped in front of her, he took her hand in his, placed his other hand on her back and there she was, dancing with Chase Mackey…

Again it wasn't quite how she'd imagined it. If this had been her daydream, both of his arms would have been around her and hers would have been around him. Not even air could have passed between them, they'd be so close, and her head would have been on his chest.

But even while none of that was the case, she still felt slightly dazed to find herself there.

Dazed and struggling to remind herself that she shouldn't be letting it affect her in any way.

Think of something to say! she commanded herself.

But all she could think about was how nice it felt to have her hand nestled in his much bigger one, to feel his other hand on her back through the satin of her bridesmaid's dress, to feel the solid muscle of his bicep, to be able to look directly up at that handsome face only inches away…

Then Chase broke the silence she hadn't been able to fill and said, "Logan said you designed and made Meg's wedding dress and all the bridesmaids' dresses."

"Design is an overstatement," Hadley demurred. "Meg wanted everyone to be in a style that made us happy, as long as all the bridesmaids' dresses were the same color. So I had everyone show me pictures of their favorite dresses. Which is also what I did for Meg. Then I just compiled styles that seemed to suit us each individually, drew them up and made them—Meg's in white satin, ours in bronze because that was the color Meg chose."

"You just did all that? That's a lot."

"It isn't really designing, though. It was more in the realm of the seamstress than the designer."

"Well, they're all great."

And that was something he'd likely noticed when he'd checked out every female there, Hadley told herself. She had to keep in mind that regardless of how much attention he might be paying her for the time being—and paying to her knee-length, curve-skimming strapless cocktail-style dress—this was still a guy whose only commitment was to playing the field.

Remembering that actually helped calm her reaction to dancing with him and, for that, she was grateful.

When the music ended again, Logan and Meg were

ready to cut the cake. The guests and the wedding party all gathered around them and the five-layer concoction. In the process Hadley's services were required to keep Tia contained so the toddler didn't swipe her fingers through the frosting.

Once that initial slice was made and pictures of it were taken, the caterer took over the cutting and serving, and while Hadley tempted the excited Tia back to the table to eat cake, Chase answered Logan's call to say hello to an old friend.

Hadley was sure that would put an end to tonight's contact with Chase. She fought her odd sense of disappointment by stealing a bite of her niece's dessert. Then she looked up just in time to see a woman approach Chase where he was talking to Logan and two other men.

Hadley recognized the woman's face but couldn't recall her name. The important thing, however, was Chase's response to her. It looked as if he didn't immediately know who the woman was, either. But when recognition dawned, his grin was blinding.

While Hadley watched, he touched the other woman's arm, leaned in and kissed her cheek and Hadley could tell even from the distance that he was just oozing charm.

And that's why you don't have to worry, Logan, she thought as she observed the exchange that was so similar to too many she'd witnessed in the past with her former husband. The opening gambit—that's what she'd come to consider it.

And she knew too well where it ended.

So no, her brother didn't have to worry that she would get involved with Chase Mackey. Even if dancing with him had given her goose bumps.

And since she'd seen enough, she turned her full attention to her niece.

Tia had finished her cake—she had more of it on her face and hands than she'd probably eaten. Hadley laughed at the sight and pulled the little girl onto her lap. "Come here and let me clean you up," she said, dipping a napkin into a water glass to wash Tia's face.

Tia squirmed and complained but a yawn in the process also told Hadley how tired the child was. Tired enough not to fight when the cleanup was complete and Hadley said, "Let's sit here for a minute and close our eyes."

That was all it took for Tia to do exactly that, to rest her head against Hadley's chest and almost instantly drop off to sleep.

The reception was coming to an end anyway, so Hadley didn't mind spending the rest of it sitting there with her sleeping niece until enough of the party had dwindled that she could duck out herself.

In order for Meg and Logan to be guaranteed an uninterrupted wedding night, Tia was sleeping over with Hadley in her apartment above the garage. When Hadley could catch the attention of her brother, she flagged him down to tell him she was taking Tia there.

Logan kissed his daughter's forehead, then said he'd see them both in the morning and returned to his bride.

Hadley gathered her niece into her arms and stood. And from out of nowhere, Chase was there again, this time reaching for Tia.

"Let me have her," he suggested.

"I'm taking her to the apartment for the night," Hadley informed him.

"I know, I heard," he responded, scooping Tia out of her arms without waking the child.

Hadley considered arguing with him, but she didn't want to risk disturbing Tia, either, so she merely conceded and she and Chase left the reception.

The showroom and the detached garage were side-by-side behind the main house. It was a short walk through the quiet of the night and neither of them said anything along the way.

Hadley led Chase up the staircase that traced the side of the garage, lit by a row of lantern-style lights that followed the same incline that the railing and steps did. When she arrived at the top she opened her door and held it for Chase to go ahead of her. She'd left a single lamp on in the roomy studio apartment so she didn't have to come home in the dark.

"You can put her on the bed," Hadley whispered when she'd followed Chase inside, waiting at the open door to let him back out again so he would know in advance that that was all that was going to come of this.

Whether he took the hint or had never intended to do anything else, he gently laid Tia on the bed that stood on a platform two steps higher than the rest of the apartment and then returned to the door where he went out onto the landing again.

He didn't leave yet, though. On the landing, he turned to face Hadley and said, "Neily said she'll be here with the baby tomorrow afternoon, probably after Logan and Meg have left."

"There'll be a cleaning crew to put the showroom in order but I promised Meg that I would pick up all the residual wedding mess at the house tomorrow, so I'll be there all day. I'm sure you have unpacking to do at your place. I can just call you when Neily gets here and you can come over then."

"That works," he agreed. His too-handsome face slid into a grin just before he said, "So, do you want to name your price now or later?"

"My price?" Hadley repeated.

"For this baby gig—I'll owe you for it."

"Actually, I'm looking at it as paying you back," she admitted.

The grin disappeared and a confused frown replaced it. "Paying me back? For what?"

Hadley looked into those blue eyes, seeing that he genuinely didn't know what she meant, and it made her smile a little as she said, "You always treated me like you didn't even see the weight. You never made fun of me. I heard you more than once tell kids who were making fun of me to stop it. And there was that time with Trinity Hatcher when he had me cornered because he wanted to feel the fat..."

It had been so long ago and yet that awful, frightening, mortifying incident still had the power to make her voice crack.

Hadley paused, feeling her smile turn sad. She didn't want Chase to see that, so she glanced downward, looking at the boards that made up the landing he was standing on rather than at him.

"You pulled him away," she went on. "You backed him up against the wall and got in his face and told him if he ever came near me again he'd have you to answer to..."

And her eyes were filling with tears? She'd thought she was so far past that. Where had tears come from?

She blinked them away and took a breath so she could finish, still unable to look up.

"I owe you for all that," she said in a voice that was softer than it had been.

"It was nothing," Chase said almost as softly and with a note in his voice that made her think he understood how hard things had been for her. Some, anyway.

She swallowed back the old emotions and finally managed to pull her head up, to meet his eyes again. "Well, this will be nothing, too," she claimed. "And then we'll be even—nothing for nothing."

He smiled at that, a tender smile as those blue eyes searched her face. He continued to study her for a moment, shaking his head at her.

Her hair had fallen forward and when she'd raised her head again, one strand hadn't gone back into place. Chase used a single index finger to smooth that strand away from the corner of her eye and the bare brush of his finger against her skin renewed those goose bumps from earlier.

But more than that, as she stood there, looking up into the face she'd filled so many lonely hours picturing in her mind, she flashed to another of her frequent fantasies from when she was a girl—the fantasy of Chase standing with her in a doorway like this, saying good-night. The fantasy of him kissing her...

Which was not going to happen.

Which she didn't want to happen.

And yet when it ran through her mind her gaze fastened on his mouth and she couldn't help wondering what it might actually be like if he did...

But in the same way that to Hadley the very idea of dancing with him had been momentous while to him it had been commonplace—Hadley knew it wasn't kissing that was on Chase's mind. And that was confirmed when he said, "I'll still beat the hell out of Hatcher if he comes anywhere near you."

Hadley knew he was joking to ease the tension and she appreciated it.

She dragged her focus from his lips to his eyes once more.

"Thanks," she said blithely to help in that attempt to lighten things.

"And on that note, I'll let you go and get some practice taking care of Tia so you'll be warmed up for the real test tomorrow," Chase said, turning to face the steps rather than her.

But before he went any farther, he glanced over his shoulder at her once more and said, "It's good to see you again, Had. I'm glad to have you onboard all the way around."

"Thanks," she whispered as he went down the stairs.

And that was when she had to admit to herself that no matter what she told Logan, no matter what she told herself, she did have a soft spot for Chase Mackey. That she probably always had. That she probably always would.

She just wasn't going to do anything about it.

Not now.

Not ever.

Not even if thoughts of kissing did flicker through her mind to torture her just a little and make that soft spot difficult to ignore.

Chapter Four

"I had no idea…"

It was late Monday night, and an extremely worn-out, frazzled Hadley had to laugh at Chase when he said that. He sighed as he handed her a bottle of beer and collapsed onto the leather sofa with one for himself.

The social worker hadn't arrived with Cody until nearly four that afternoon. She had handed off the baby, his things and instructions from the foster mother. She had also warned Hadley and Chase that given the fact that in the past ten days he'd lost his mother and been shuffled from home to home, Cody was apt to cry.

And that's what he'd been doing ever since. Inconsolably. Fearfully. Pitifully. Loudly.

He'd cried while Chase had maneuvered Tia's old

crib into the loft's second bedroom and reassembled it. He'd cried while they'd unpacked his things and set up Tia's old changing table. He'd cried rather than eat the jarred food that had been sent with him from his foster home. He'd cried despite being held, walked, rocked, jiggled, sung and talked to. He'd cried through his bath and diaper changes. He'd cried harder when Chase had tried to hold him, he'd cried even when Hadley had attempted to give him a bottle. He'd just cried until he'd finally cried himself to sleep a few minutes earlier.

"I never knew quiet could sound so good," Chase said, sinking low enough to rest his head on the cushion behind him.

Chase had talked Hadley into staying for a beer, insisting that after what they'd been through with the baby, they could both use one. Hadley knew that the real reason he wanted her there was in case Cody woke up again. She'd agreed for the same reason. Or so she told herself.

She was sitting on a love seat that matched his sofa. It was still positioned where the movers had left it—facing the couch—and there were only inches between the two pieces of furniture. When Chase put his feet up onto the love seat beside her, she put hers onto the sofa beside him.

"Poor little guy," she said.

"Him or me?" Chase asked wryly, making her laugh again.

"Him. He doesn't know us, he doesn't understand

what's happening or where his mom is—he must be so scared and discombobulated."

"Discombobulated?" Chase repeated, the word finally bringing a slight smile to a face that had been almost forlorn ever since this afternoon.

"Yes, discombobulated—confused, disoriented. That poor baby doesn't know what's going on."

"All I know is that his mother said he was a good baby—no trouble at all—and I can't wait for that to kick in."

"Was that what she said on the DVD? I've been wondering what was on that."

"It was just a woman named Angie Cragen sitting in front of her computer, talking."

"About Cody?"

"Along with a lot of other stuff."

Other stuff that drew deeper frown lines between Chase's brows as Hadley watched him and wondered if he was going to tell her what that other stuff might be.

She wished he would. Whatever that DVD contained, it seemed as if talking about it might give her a distraction that she sorely needed. The jeans and white crewneck T-shirt that Chase was wearing accentuated his every asset. Plus, there was the shadow of a beard making an evening reappearance that gave him an even more rugged handsomeness, and despite the fact that it was clear he'd been run through the wringer in the past several hours, he somehow still managed to have an intense sex appeal that Hadley kept trying to ignore.

Chase took a long drink of his beer and then got up again. The loft had an open flow between the living room, the kitchen and the dining room, with only the bathroom and two bedrooms walled in for privacy. The entire place was in just-moving-in condition, which made today more chaotic, not only with what had come with Cody, but also with an abundance of Tia's old baby things brought over by Logan before he, Meg and Tia had left on their honeymoon trip.

Chase went to the dining table and rummaged through some of the rubble before returning to hand Hadley what he'd retrieved from the debris.

As he sat down again, he said, "I found that in the envelope with the DVD. Neily must not have known it was there. It's a picture of all five kids taken somewhere here in town just before we were orphaned."

Hadley looked at it. It was a posed, professional photograph of a girl who looked to be about seven or eight sitting amidst four much, much younger children—Chase, who looked enough like he did now to be recognizable, a little girl who was barely more than a toddler and twin newborn infants.

"I remember doing this with my family," Hadley said as she studied the photo. "The Dunlaps had a photography studio set up in their basement for a while. When we were kids we had pictures taken there, too, with this same country-scene background. And this has to be you—those blue eyes are a dead giveaway, and you even had that dent in your chin then."

"Yeah, I guess it is me, but I don't have the slightest recollection of it."

"And seeing it didn't spur any memory of the other kids in it?"

"None."

"But it is sort of proof…" Hadley pointed out, setting the photograph on the coffee table that was haphazardly placed next to the love seat. "It's you and your brothers and sisters…"

"Seems like it," Chase conceded. "According to what this Angie said on the DVD, I was the first kid born after her mother married my father. She was five years old then."

"How did Angie seem?"

Chase shrugged. "Really weak and ill—she had one of those oxygen tubes in her nose even on the DVD. Apparently she met Cody's father at her cardiologist's office—I'll bet no one thought of that as a place to hook up."

Hadley made a face. "I know I never have. So Cody came from two sick parents—maybe you should have him checked out medically."

"Angie said he has been. He's perfectly healthy."

"That's lucky," Hadley said. "And obviously Angie made it through his birth, but then…" she said to keep Chase going.

"The birth took a toll on her heart that she couldn't bounce back from," Chase said. "I guess she was on the heart-transplant list, but a month ago she decided she had to start accepting that she might not make it long enough to find a donor and had better make provisions for Cody. That's when she decided to start trying to find her lost brothers and sister—"

"You, the little girl and the twins in the picture."

"Right."

"And you were the one she found," Hadley said, putting her half-empty beer bottle on the coffee table.

Chase finished his own beer and set the bottle down. Then he sat back and faced her. "It's like Neily said— because I was never adopted, my name was still Mackey and that's where Angie started looking. She found the Mackey and McKendrick Web site and did some research using the newspaper and magazine articles that have been written about us. Plus our pictures are on the Web site—she saw the resemblance you saw."

"So she got that far but couldn't actually make contact with you?" Hadley asked.

"I left New York three weeks ago. Apparently Angie called our offices after I was already gone. I guess when she spoke to our secretary she told her that she was my sister. But our secretary knew I didn't have a sister and… well, I've had a pretty active social life—sometimes women come out of the woodwork either to meet me or because I bought them a drink or just looked at them at a club or something. Our secretary sort of guards the gates so not everyone gets by and I think that's what happened."

"Only this time it wasn't one of your groupies trying

to get by the guard at the gate, it was your half sister," Hadley pointed out.

"Groupies?" he repeated with a laugh.

"That's what it sounds like to me," Hadley confirmed.

"I don't know about that. But yeah. I guess a further call from the lawyer got the information that I was no longer based in New York, that I was relocating here. But Angie couldn't hang on long enough for me to get here to talk to me herself."

Essentially his social life had cost him ever knowing his half sister. But Hadley didn't say that. Instead she said, "It's sad that you came so close to meeting her and didn't get to."

"There's not much in this whole thing that isn't sad," he said. "Anyway, Angie had the lawyer do a background check on me that let her know I don't have any kind of criminal record or any history that might make me a danger to her kid."

"But she didn't know about your social life…" Hadley said before thinking better of it.

That made him look amused and confused at once. "Meaning that even though nothing bad shows up in a background check I'm still unfit?"

"No, I'm just saying that she didn't know that your lifestyle doesn't really allow for being a father."

"My lifestyle? You make that sound really unsavory."

"The active social life that has so many women

tracking you down that you have to have a guard at the gate to weed them out," she qualified. "It's a giant leap from that to playing dad."

"Today was definitely a giant leap from what I'm used to, I'll give you that," he allowed.

And Hadley thought she might have insulted him, so she changed the subject. "Did your half sister talk about anything else on the DVD? Did she tell you anything about your parents?"

"She talked about the accident. We were new to Northbridge and our folks had left us with a babysitter while they went out for their anniversary. The babysitter was just a teenager from next door, so when the accident happened, the police came and took the five of us to a man Angie didn't remember well—she thought he was a priest or a minister or something—"

"That would have been Reverend Perry, then, wouldn't it?"

Chase shrugged. "I suppose."

"And you don't remember any of it?"

"None. It's a complete blank."

"I know that Neily said just in passing that before her, Northbridge didn't have its own social worker. I suppose that's why you would have been taken to the reverend. I guess he'd be the next best thing to handle something like that in a small town."

"I called Angie's lawyer early this morning for more information but he wouldn't tell me anything over the phone. I made an appointment with him for tomorrow—in Billings. Before I had any idea what it would be like to deal with Cody..."

Chase shook his head before continuing, "Anyway, Angie loved that kid..."

"Which was why she tried to make sure he was taken care of by the only family she had."

"Right. Me or if not me, she said she hoped that I would go on to find the other sister and the twins, that maybe one of them would take him if I didn't want to." Chase smiled a wry, one-sided smile. "Maybe she had an idea about what kind of lifestyle I lead and she knew a kid wouldn't fit into it."

"Do you think a kid will fit into it?" Hadley asked.

"After the last few hours? I don't think all that crying would fit into anybody's life...or lifestyle," he said, without actually answering her question.

Still, her own curiosity caused her to push him a little and she said, "Are you going to try to find your other brothers and sister to see if they'll take him?"

Because that was what she was betting he would do, even as a part of her held out hope that he might accept the responsibility for his nephew—although why she should care, she didn't know....

"I'll probably try to find them," he said.

Chase got to his feet and headed for the refrigerator. "Want another beer?"

"I didn't finish this one," Hadley admitted. "And it's getting late. I think Cody will stay asleep for the night now so I should go home."

And yet she wasn't eager to...

"Wait...was that him?" Chase pretended to hear something, cocking an ear in the direction of the bedroom they'd set up for the baby.

"You know it wasn't," Hadley said, laughing at him and standing before she let herself be persuaded to stay.

"Tomorrow—"

"I know," Hadley cut him off, "I'd better be here the minute Cody wakes up in the morning. Or were you going to say that you want to give it a try on your own?"

"No!" Chase answered in mock panic that Hadley knew had a little of the real thing behind it. "In fact, if you wanted to stay the night you could have my bed and I'd sleep out here on the couch. Because what if he wakes up in the night? He still hasn't let me near enough to even try to change a diaper. He likes you better than me, and if I'm the one who goes into his room—"

"I'm not staying the night," Hadley said, though the moment he'd mentioned it she had actually been tempted.

And not for the sake of Cody....

"I'll be right next door," she assured. "Even if he wakes up in the night you can call me and I'll be here in two minutes. The same goes for the morning—if he wakes up earlier than his instructions say he usually does, just call me. Otherwise, I'll try to be here right about then."

"You're really going to leave me alone here all night with the screamer?"

Hadley laughed at him as she headed for the door. "The screamer?" she repeated. "He's only a baby and he's just—"

"I know—discombobulated."

"Something I'm thinking you might be able to relate to…" she teased him as he came back from the kitchen section of the loft to join her at the door.

The remark made him smile, and he had such a great smile that it tempted her all over again to just go ahead and stay.

But there was no way she could do that, she told herself firmly.

"You'll be fine," she said.

"One peep out of him and I'm calling," he warned.

"Understood."

"Oh, but what about tomorrow?" he suddenly remembered. "That appointment with the lawyer in Billings is in the afternoon. When I made it I was thinking that maybe I could get you to just stay with the screamer while I went. But now that I know what he's like, it doesn't seem fair to leave you alone with him, and I know I can't take him to Billings on my own. So what would you say to the three of us going together? If he's being bad maybe you can deal with him in the waiting room while I talk to the lawyer, but otherwise neither of us will be alone with him—it seems easier to take that way."

Hadley knew she could stay home with Cody and manage on her own. But Chase was right, dealing with the unhappy baby was slightly easier when there were two of them. And Cody did need to be around Chase in order to get more familiar with him—she wouldn't be doing either of them a service to interfere with that. Plus Chase needed lessons in putting the car seat in the car, in putting the baby in the car seat, in taking the baby out in public. And Cody might even be better on a car ride. And...

And who was she kidding? She didn't want to be left behind to babysit when she could take a short road trip with Chase on a beautiful autumn day.

"Okay," she said simply enough. "I'll go."

That made him grin. "So I'm not the only one who doesn't want to do this kid thing alone," he said, interpreting her choice.

"I may not want to, but at least I could if I had to—can you say that?" she challenged.

"The kid hates me, I can't help it," Chase joked.

"Which is something else we need to work on tomorrow. I don't think he hates you, I think he senses that he scares you to death and that makes him scared, too."

"Scares me to death?"

"Deny it," she dared.

"Okay, he scares me to death," Chase acknowledged with another grin.

For a moment he just went on like that—grinning down at her. Then he said, "It helps, though, that I'm having a good time with you. And I like that we have the chance to get to know each other all grown up. Even if it was me doing the talking tonight, I want to know about you, too."

"Who wouldn't? I *am* fascinating," she said glibly.

"You say that as if you don't believe it, but I think there's a lot more to you than you're letting on and I can't wait to uncover it all..."

Was he insinuating something? And was that grin of his suddenly shaded with a hint of sexiness?

There was no place for sexiness in their new relationship, she insisted to herself. She would not let herself become the first woman in Northbridge to occupy Chase Mackey's wandering eye before it wandered elsewhere.

Except that even as she was thinking that, another part of her was once more remembering that youthful fantasy of him kissing her. That same fantasy that had lingered as she'd undressed and gone to bed last night, when it had somehow changed into a whole new one of the Chase of now kissing the Hadley of now...

And then Chase leaned forward and actually did kiss her.

On the cheek.

Right before he said, "Go on, rest up for the assault on your eardrums that tomorrow will no doubt bring."

In a bit of a daze, Hadley nodded. "You, too."

Then she left to walk next door to her own place, thinking as she did: A kiss on the cheek?

A kiss on the cheek was what any of her brothers or a friend might have given her.

A sister or a friend—that was how Chase viewed her.

Which was exactly as it should have been.

Exactly as it had been a hundred pounds ago.

Nothing had changed....

Not that she'd come into this thinking that the weight loss was going to make Chase take one look at her and fall instantly in love. That wasn't even what she wanted.

It was just...

She wasn't exactly sure what it was.

Maybe it would have been nice to think that resisting her was even just a little difficult for Chase.

But a kiss on the cheek? That was a sign that Chase saw her no differently than he had all those years ago—heavy or not so heavy.

Only now she didn't even have those extra hundred pounds to blame it on.

"He just doesn't see you the way he sees other women," she told herself as she went into her apartment.

But why not?

From as much as he'd played around in high school, from all the things she'd heard about him from Logan over the years, Chase Mackey was a man who seemed to want every woman.

Every woman except her.

And no matter how strongly she believed that anything happening between them would be a mistake, no matter how determined she was not to get involved with—and eventually hurt by—another skirt-chaser, she at least wanted Chase to want her the way he did every other woman.

Even if he couldn't have her.

Chapter Five

"What do you say, big guy? Will you let me carry you to the car?"

Chase was holding out his hands to Cody the way Hadley had shown him. The eleven-month-old baby was sitting up on the changing table. Hadley had just finished dressing him for the drive to Billings and had stepped to one side to free the way for Chase.

Cody was staring solemnly at Chase with big brown eyes. He had his thumb in his mouth, and despite all attempts to comb it down, his champagne-colored hair insisted on spiking upward on top.

But at least he wasn't crying—the morning had had less of that, more of him warming up to Hadley while still staring suspiciously at Chase and threatening to cry again whenever Chase got near him.

Hadley was trying to encourage a connection between the two of them. She'd counseled Chase to just offer to pick Cody up, to let Cody consent to contact before putting hands on him.

"Then we can go bye-bye," Hadley tempted.

Cody looked at her as if that was not enough of an incentive.

"Oh, I guess for someone who's been moved around as much as he has that's more scary than fun, isn't it?" she said under her breath to Chase.

When the infant merely went back to staring at Chase, Hadley tried another tack.

"It's all right, Cody, Chase is okay."

"Okay? That's the best you can do? I'm okay?" Chase pretended to be miffed by her faint praise.

Hadley wanted to say that that was the best a kiss on the cheek bought him, but she didn't. Instead she added, "Chase won't hurt you."

"Not much better," Chase whispered.

"I'm just trying to get an eleven-month-old to trust you enough to let you take him out to the car, I'm not writing a personal ad for you."

"Good thing—I'd never get a date with he's okay and won't hurt you."

That made her laugh, drawing Cody's attention back to her. He was beginning to look to her for reassurance, as if she were becoming his home base.

Given that role, she had to prove she had confidence in Chase herself, so she took a step nearer to him and said, "I like Chase."

Chase grinned at her. "You do?" he said, teasing her.

Rather than address that, Hadley spoke again to the baby. "I know he can be kind of full of himself, but he really is nice."

"Hey! I'm not full of myself. But I am nice—you could say that with more conviction."

Chase was clearly enjoying himself but Cody merely cast Hadley another uncertain glance, his bottom lip jutting out in a pout that let them both know he wasn't having as good a time as his uncle was.

"Ohhh, it's all right, sweetheart," Hadley said quickly, opting for more drastic measures by hooking her elbow around one of Chase's outstretched arms and leaning into him slightly. "I'm not afraid of him and you don't need to be, either."

Physical contact caused a whole slew of reactions in Hadley that she hadn't expected. She was suddenly overly aware of the feel of that muscular arm grasped in hers, of the power in it, the strength, of the fact that she had the instant urge to have it wrapped around her....

Cody looked at her suspiciously again, though, so—for the sake of both herself and the infant—she let go of Chase and returned to merely standing beside the big man.

Chase nodded in her direction then and tried cajoling.

"Come on, buddy, don't make me look bad in front of a girl I'm trying to impress. Be a guy...."

Chase was trying to impress her?

He did look good in a pair of slacks and a crisp white shirt, and he smelled wonderful, too—of that fresh-mountain-air cologne he'd had on at the wedding. But he'd dressed up for the meeting with the lawyer, not for her. On the other hand, she had had him in mind when she made sure that the khaki pants she'd opted for hugged her rear end to perfection, that the T-shirt she wore underneath the lacy overblouse gave her breasts a boost and that her hair was washed to a glimmering sheen.

"Be a guy?" she repeated with a laugh. "I don't think he knows what it is to be a guy at eleven months."

"Give a guy a break?" Chase amended with a side-ways gaze at her that might have been flirtatious.

Ignoring Chase, she spoke solely to Cody again. "Please, sweetheart? Let Chase pick you up."

The baby merely went on staring in stalemate, no more persuaded by Hadley's request than by Chase's attempts at camaraderie.

"Wait! I just remembered something!" Chase said then, spinning around to go to the boxes of Cody's things that had yet to be unpacked.

While Hadley gave Cody a one-armed hug and kissed the side of his head, they both watched Chase search through the boxes.

"Last night after you left, Had, I was reading through

those instructions the foster mother sent. I just remembered there was something about a favorite toy…"

Hadley really did try not to look at Chase's rear end
as he bent over the boxes. But what was she supposed
to do when there it was, taut and perfect and the only
thing to see when her eyes followed him? When one of
nature's works of art was right in front of her for her to
admire?

And admire it she did, thinking that as good as it had
been to feel his arm, feeling his derriere might be even
better.

"Here!" Chase said victoriously, straightening up
with a raggedy-looking stuffed moose with floppy legs
and antlers and a big black nose.

"Oose!" Cody exclaimed as if Chase had unearthed
a long lost friend. Cody finally did what they'd been
trying to get him to do before—he held out his arms
for the toy. He leaned so far forward that had Hadley
not been there to hang on to him he would have fallen
off the changing table.

"Oose is moose!" Hadley said as light dawned. It was
something Cody had repeated and repeated all through
his crying and they hadn't been sure if it was a word or
merely a sound the baby made.

"Oose," Cody said again.

"And see who found him for you?" Hadley pointed
out. "Chase did. I told you he was a nice man."

Chase brought the stuffed toy to the changing table
and did a maneuver where he handed the moose to Cody

at the same time he picked the baby up. Cody was in such rapture at having his toy that he didn't balk.

"Poor baby, that isn't just his favorite toy, that's like his security blanket—he must have been missing it something fierce," Hadley observed. "That shouldn't have been packed in a box, Cody should have had it with him the whole time."

"The system," Chase said critically. "Not a lot of attention to detail."

"Rescuing the Oose helped you out, though," Hadley noted as Cody settled against Chase's broad chest, cuddling the moose and putting his thumb in his mouth again as if he'd finally reached some sort of satisfactory comfort level.

Chase looked surprisingly at ease with a baby in his arms—and sexy in an altogether different way than he had before.

But Hadley definitely didn't want to be thinking about that.

So when Chase rested his blue eyes on her and said, "Okay, what do you say we get going?" she jumped at the chance to get her mind off this exasperating man.

With the stuffed moose for company, Cody made the drive to Billings fairly well. A few miles outside North-bridge, Hadley and Chase learned that playing music also helped keep him calm, so that's what they did, even though it prevented them from talking much.

"Ug!" Cody exclaimed the minute he set eyes on the

attorney they were scheduled to meet, before Hadley or Chase even realized who it was.

Douglas Atview answered the baby's greeting equally as warmly, taking Cody from Hadley when the infant leaned toward him with arms outstretched.

"Ug?" Chase repeated.

"It's the best he can do with Doug," the lawyer explained before he formally introduced himself.

"And you have to be Chase Mackey," Doug Atview said. Then looking at Hadley, he added, "Is this Mrs. Mackey?"

Hadley laughed reflexively. It sounded so strange to have someone call her that. It was something from her adolescent daydreams.

Chase corrected the mistake. "This is Hadley Mc-Kendrick," he said.

The lawyer suggested they hold their meeting in a coffee shop on the ground floor of the building. He led the way, explaining as they went, "I was doing Angie's work pro bono. Actually, she and I were next-door neighbors growing up. She was one of my best friends and her death was such a loss to me that I can't even begin to tell you. She was a wonderful, wonderful person and she loved this little guy like you can't believe. We talked about my taking him, but I'm in a blended family situation as it is—my wife has four kids from her first marriage, I have three, and Angie didn't want to add Cody to the circus at our house. I think she was afraid he'd get lost in the mix. And it was really important to her that he end up with some kind of family connection."

"Cody's dad…" Chase said as they got three coffees, a juice for Cody and sat at a small bistro table in the coffee shop.

"Peter wasn't well either—they met—"

"I know, at their doctor's office," Chase interjected. "It was on the DVD."

"Right. Poor health—a lousy thing to have in common. But they were crazy about each other and they got a few good years in before Cody's dad died. That same month Angie found out she was pregnant."

"And her doctor didn't advise against having the baby?" Hadley asked.

"He did," the attorney confirmed. "Especially since Angie was almost thirty-nine along with having health problems. But Angie wanted a child so much she was willing to take the risk. And believe me, even when she was dying, she didn't regret it."

After a glance down at Cody—who was sitting on the lawyer's lap, playing contentedly with his tie—Doug said, "I wish you could have known her. She was always so upbeat, so funny. Her health kept her down physically, but it never dragged down her spirit. She didn't dwell on it. She didn't let it be the only thing she was about…"

After a moment during which the attorney seemed lost in memory, he glanced at Chase again. "She always felt bad that her father wouldn't take you and her other brothers and sister in when he took her, after your parents were killed in that accident. But Bud—her dad—was in and out of work. He was good with Angie but outside of the house he had a temper that would cost him job after job. He was barely able to make ends meet and keep up with Angie's medical bills. She understood that he couldn't take on four more kids to boot, but she hated that you all just disappeared from her life. I think trying to find you all at the end, hoping one of you would raise Cody, was her way of reconnecting."

"On the DVD, Angie mentioned that her own dad died last year and that Cody's father didn't have family, either," Chase said then.

"Right. So without one of her half siblings taking him—"

"He would go into the system," Chase finished.

"Angie always worried about you and the others. About what had happened to *you* in the system. She hoped you'd all gone to good families, to good homes—"

"And do you know what happened to the twins and the other girl?" Chase asked, cutting the lawyer off.

Doug Atview shrugged. "Nothing, really. The most I found out was that you were all left with a Reverend Armand Perry in Northbridge. If I were you—and you're interested in finding them—I'd go to him."

The attorney turned more somber again then and said, "Are you against keeping Cody yourself?"

"I'm just taking it a day at a time at this point," Chase

answered. "But there's not only the issue of Cody. Now that I know there actually were brothers and a sister, yeah, I'm curious…"

Cody was not at all happy to leave Doug Atview behind. To make the return trip to Northbridge without too much delay—and to calm the baby again—Hadley spent part of the drive sitting in the backseat with him, feeding him dinner while Chase drove. She and Chase ate fast food they bought at a drive-through along the way. During the trip, they once more played music, which prevented too much conversation. But even if that hadn't been the case, Chase seemed particularly disinclined from talking.

By the time they arrived back home, Hadley could tell Chase needed some time on his own. She suggested he skip the second evening's lesson on bathing Cody and instead get started on the chore she knew he was eager to do—unload the moving truck that had stalled on him on Saturday and recently been repaired and brought in. He jumped at the idea and so Hadley got Cody bathed and ready for bed by herself.

But once she was finished with that it was still slightly early for putting the baby down, so with Cody dressed in his footy pajamas and carrying his stuffed moose, she took him to where Chase worked downstairs with the moving truck backed up to the showroom's delivery doors.

"Wow, you're making headway," she said when she

surveyed the truck and discovered that it was a third empty already.

"I'm just moving the smaller stuff. The bigger pieces will have to wait for help. And what I do take off I'm only setting aside. I figure Logan and I can bring everything from here onto the showroom floor later on."

Hadley perched on a moving crate and propped Cody on her lap where both of them watched Chase strap a solid oak bookcase that looked as if it could take up space in an old English library to a dolly.

"I wasn't sure you could do this alone," she said, taking in the sight of him as he worked.

He'd changed clothes before getting started and was wearing ragged jeans and a plain T-shirt more suited to furniture moving. More suited to exhibiting the muscles in his legs and every rippling sinew of his torso and arms, too.

He cast Cody a wink as if the two were sharing an inside joke. Then he said, "Our boy looks content."

"Tonight is definitely better than last night. He must be getting used to things."

Chase studied them both as he walked the bookshelf-laden dolly down the ramp.

"That's kind of a nice picture—the two of you like that," he said as he reached the bottom of the ramp.

"Too bad Mr. Dunlap isn't around to take our picture," she joked, referring to the photographer who had taken Chase's and her own family's portraits.

"Funny, I was just thinking about him," Chase said

as he unstrapped the bookcase. "He did those pictures hanging on that wall alongside the stairs at your parents' house, didn't he. I remember there being one of you and Logan, one of you and Logan with your dad, and one of your dad and your stepmother with the other kids—but not one of all of you together."

"Because there wasn't one of all of us together," Hadley said. "My stepmother didn't consider Logan and me to be real McKendricks."

"Yeah…seems like I remember that. Logan would say that you two were second-class citizens to your stepmother. I thought it was just stepparent resentment or something, but she really didn't even let you into the family picture?"

"That was the smallest of the things she did. I wasn't even three years old when she married my dad—she would have been the only real mother I knew except that she always made a point of telling me she wasn't my mother. I can remember thinking when I was a little, little kid that if she could have waved a magic wand and made Logan and me disappear, she would have. She did not like raising another woman's kids and she made sure we knew it. We could never do anything right in her eyes, and when it came to me, there was a lot for her to find fault with."

"Why?" Chase asked as he positioned the bookcase just so and removed the dolly from underneath it.

"Because Logan was a boy and Sandra didn't think boys should have to do anything domestic, Logan didn't get as much dumped on him as I did," Hadley explained. "But me? By the time I was four years old she was putting me to work. She said that a girl had to know what to do around the house—that seemed to give her license to make me her live-in maid, cook, babysitter, laundress—you name it, it was my job, even long after Tessa, Issa and Zeli were old enough to pitch in, too."

"You were Cinderella?" Chase joked. But there was some empathy in his tone that made it tolerable. And it didn't hurt that as he took the dolly back into the truck just then Hadley got a view of his rear end that sent a wave of appreciation through her.

"Cinderella and the wicked stepmother—you're teasing but it applies," Hadley said in a voice that was raspier than she wished it had been.

"Now that you mention it, it was always you setting the table and putting the food on it and doing dishes afterwards and then shuffling the younger kids to bed. What about your dad? Didn't he step in?"

"When he noticed that I was working like a dog and said something to her, she told him that girls needed to know how to do whatever it was she was making me do, and that would be the end of it."

"So what about the other kids—your half sisters and brothers—it always seemed like you were all pretty close, but I'd think there would be some resentment…" Chase said.

"We were close, and Logan and I didn't resent them or blame them for what their mother did."

"She sure was tough on you about your weight," Chase said as he wheeled down a classic country-style armoire with beadboard detailing.

"She was vicious," Hadley said. "And then in that irrational way kids can act, I'd eat all the more to spite her."

Chase's eyebrows arched at that bit of revelation. "So when you got away from her the weight just disappeared?"

"I wish!" Hadley said with a quiet laugh because Cody was falling asleep in her arms and she didn't want to disturb him. "No, the weight didn't just disappear but losing it was a lot easier once I was out from under Sandra's nastiness. After I left home I had some counseling that helped me see some of the reasons I was overeating. Leaving her behind also left behind most of the reasons I'd gorged myself, so I was able to turn things around. Plus, rather than doing anything crazy or faddish, I just adopted a more moderate diet that didn't make me feel deprived—chocolate was still on the menu, just less of it," she added with a laugh.

"But you had to go all the way to Europe to get far enough away to do all that?" he asked.

"I didn't go instantly from Northbridge to Europe," Hadley amended. "The first place I went was to art school in Chicago."

"Now see, that I never knew about you when we were kids—that you were artistic," he said as he unstrapped the armoire and took the dolly back to the truck. "When Logan told me you were going to art school I was surprised."

"I wanted to be a fashion designer," Hadley said. "My stepmother thought it was a great irony that that was what a fat girl aspired to."

Chase flinched for her.

Hadley laughed at him. "Yeah, I think I ate a whole pizza when she said that. But it was my portfolio that got me accepted, no one cared how much I weighed—which, again, was such a blessing. To be seen as the person I am, for my talents and abilities, rather than how much I weighed, was sort of freeing."

Back in the truck, Chase picked up a small dining table with a beautifully carved pedestal at its center and carried it down. That provided an even better show of broad shoulders flexing and biceps bulging into high definition.

While Hadley was trying not to feast on the sight, Chase said, "I hate to admit it, but I kind of thought I knew you and now I'm figuring out that I really don't. And not only that, as close as I've always been to Logan and as much as we see of each other, as much as we talk, we didn't discuss you much. So what did you do right after school?"

"I went to Italy—mainly Milan—after graduating. I sewed haute couture there for seven years. Which is a fancy way of saying I became a seamstress. Primarily for someone else…"

That someone else being her ex-husband. But she

was enjoying sitting there, holding a very mellow Cody and updating Chase on the steps that had led her to this point. She didn't want to get into talking about her former spouse or her divorce.

"Huh," Chase said.

"I also learned to eat the European way—"

"Which is?"

"It's all about quality food. It's about taking time to truly enjoy what you're eating. And the company you're sharing while you do. It wasn't so much just stuffing something fast in my mouth on the run."

"And then Paris?" Chase asked.

"Paris…" Hadley said dreamily. "I loved Paris. I worked haute couture there, too, and really honed my craft…" Before the city, the country and the atmosphere of the work itself were irreparably damaged for her…

"And now you're going to sew seat cushions for us?" Chase asked with even more confusion.

The answer to that, too, would have brought her ex into the conversation, so Hadley merely said, "I got tired of the fashion industry and everything that went with it. I'm looking at this as a chance to get back in touch with the textile end of things. Maybe add a little flash and flair and panache to the upholstery portions of your designs."

"I like that idea. I just hope you don't get bored with us," Chase said.

He'd finished unloading as much as he could alone from the truck and as he crossed the distance between them he was looking down and brushing something Hadley couldn't see off of his jeans. Off of his upper thigh. Very near his zipper.

Flustered, she ended up saying, "Oh, I can't imagine being bored with you…"

And she said it in a much more breathless voice than she wished she had.

What it all amounted to was a devilishly knowing grin on Chase's face when she forced her eyes away from his jeans.

"Well, I'll certainly see what I can do…" he said with a voice full of insinuation.

Hadley didn't blush easily but she could feel her cheeks heating.

With nowhere to run, she pretended an intent interest in Cody and dropped her head far forward to look at him. And to change the subject.

"Sound asleep," she said, her voice cracking now and only making things worse. "I might as well put him in his crib and get home."

"Let me carry him," Chase offered.

But Hadley knew that would mean Chase slipping his hands between the slumbering infant and the front of her, coming into contact with her, and she was too afraid that might make things worse.

So she got down from the crate and moved out of Chase's reach in a hurry. "We don't want to risk waking him. It's better if he stays like this and I just put him in the crib myself."

The glimmer of amusement in Chase's sky-blue eyes made it clear that he knew she was rattled. But he only said, "I'll follow you, then."

Neither of them uttered a word as they went to the staircase that led to the loft. But with Chase going up the stairs behind her, Hadley worried the whole way where his eyes might be. She was glad when they'd made it and were side by side again.

Cody remained sound asleep—his moose still grasped tightly in one arm—as she laid him in the crib and covered him. Then, with Chase trailing her, Hadley went out of the baby's bedroom and straight to the loft's main door to leave, ignoring the sudden urge not to. But watching Chase work had roused too many unwanted inclinations in her and she knew that to be safe, she had to get out of there.

"Remember, I'm going to see Reverend Perry tomorrow to get him to tell us anything he might know about my lost sister and brothers." Chase said as he went with her to the door.

"Right," Hadley confirmed.

"Don't forget you promised you'd go—that guy never liked me."

"That guy doesn't like anybody. But he's harmless—you saw him at Meg and Logan's wedding—he's just a cranky old man now."

"What I'm hoping is that he'll be less cranky with you there—you're in-laws now that Logan married his granddaughter."

"Don't bet on it."

"But you'll still go, right?"

As with going to Billings, she knew she should beg off and stay at home to babysit Cody. But she was no more inclined to be put in the babysitter slot now than she had been yesterday. So she said, "Yes, I will still go. To help wrestle Cody if he's bad, and as your moral support."

"Moral support..." he repeated with satisfaction. "I like that."

He'd reached the door slightly ahead of her and was leaning one shoulder against the jamb, facing Hadley. He wasn't actually barricading the door, but he was in the way enough that opening it with him there would have grazed him. It was awkward.

Hadley wondered if he'd positioned himself like that on purpose. But why? Did the way he was studying her, the way he was smiling that secret little smile have anything to do with it?

She stalled, hoping he'd get out of the way. "It seems like you ended up in a better mood tonight than you were in on the way home from Billings."

"Being with you seems to do that to me—put me in a better mood than I start out in."

"Or you're just happy that I let you off the hook with Cody tonight."

His smile turned into a grin again. "That, too," he confirmed. "Anything I can do to put off learning to change a diaper is a win."

"I'm sorry to tell you, but your time is up—now that he's gone from terrified of you to just leery, your real lessons in babycare are about to begin."

He nodded but the way he continued to look at her made her think he was only partially paying attention to what they were talking about, that something else was on his mind.

Then he proved that by saying, "Your stepmother couldn't have been more wrong about you."

Hadley frowned slightly. "I don't know where that came from, but there wasn't much my stepmother was right about, especially about me. But what are you thinking specifically?"

"Making you feel worthless and ugly. You're definitely not worthless—I don't know what I'd be doing without you right now. Plus you're talented and smart and…" He shook his head. "And ugly? Wow…you are sooo not ugly. It would be much easier for me if you were. But instead I'm just blown away every time I look at you. I guess I'm just blown away by you all the way around."

So blown away that he'd kissed her on the cheek last night?

"I should get going," she said, her voice soft and a little sad sounding, although she doubted he would pick up on that. Or on why.

And she shouldn't be sounding sad or feeling sad, she lectured herself. Kissing wasn't on her agenda with this man and she needed to stop thinking about it. Wishing for it. Resenting it when all he did was kiss her on the cheek…

Chase didn't move an inch despite her pointing out that she should get going. And he didn't take his eyes off of her, either.

So Hadley placed her hand on the doorknob.

Still he didn't back up. Instead he raised a hand to the side of her neck.

Don't you dare kiss me on the cheek again as if I'm someone's old aunt or grandmother!

But this was obviously different. Especially when he inched his hand into her hair, when his thumb began making soft circles on her jawbone, when the look in his eyes was warm and maybe a little primal.

Then he tilted her head back just a bit and in he came, aiming not for her cheek tonight, but pressing his mouth to hers in a kiss no one would give an old aunt or grandmother.

His lips were parted, silky and smooth, and they took hers in a way that was purely sensual. A way that was nothing at all like she'd imagined as a girl. This was much, much better.

And oh, boy, did she kiss him back! Out of nothing but instinct and for no other reason than that she wanted to.

Too soon it was over, though, and Chase was gazing down at her again, looking a little as if he'd just indulged in a guilty pleasure.

But he didn't say anything. He merely pivoted so that

his back was flat against the wall, leaving the doorway perfectly clear, watching her from beneath hooded eyes since he'd also tipped his head to the wall.

It took Hadley a moment to recover her wits. To realize he wasn't going to say anything.

She knew she should. That she should chastise him and take him to task for that kiss. That she should tell him never, ever to do it again. That that wasn't the sort of relationship they were ever going to have.

But none of those words would come and so she finally just opened the door.

"I'll see you in the morning," she barely whispered.

Chase did nothing but nod his head, his gaze remaining on her as she went out into the cool September air.

And as she crossed the yard tonight she reminded herself that everything about Chase that made him appealing to her was exactly what made him appealing to other women, too.

You can't let him get to you! she told herself in no uncertain terms.

If she did, she knew it would be fun and flattering for a while, and then miserable for her when he went on to the next woman in line—as she had no doubt he would.

And yet when she let herself into her apartment those thoughts somehow evaporated and all she was really thinking was that Chase Mackey had kissed her.

A genuine kiss.

On the mouth.

A kiss that had been exceptional in spite of the ending coming sooner than she wished it had.

An exceptional kiss from her former fantasy man...

The one man she was not supposed to be kissing....

Chapter Six

"Baby in the kitchen!"

Hadley was coming out of one of the bathrooms in Chase's loft when Chase yelled. "I just put him down for a second while I washed my hands—how did he get all the way out here that quick?"

"The kid can move when he wants to," Chase said.

Chase was standing at the stove and he nodded downward as Hadley rounded the center island. Cody had crawled to the cupboard and discovered he could open the door and pull pots and pans out.

"Come here, you little bugger," she said. "I'm not putting those pans away again. Besides, it's your bedtime."

Hadley scooped Cody up into her arms and then

turned to Chase. "It definitely smells better in here than where I came from," she said.

"I'd take that as a compliment except that you just came from changing a diaper."

Chase made that comment with a smile—the first one Hadley had seen from him since their meeting with Reverend Perry that afternoon.

The visit had been productive. They'd garnered some information from the Reverend about where he'd placed Chase's siblings all those years ago.

At the time, two young couples had come forward— Lila and Tony Bruno had taken the two-month-old twin boys, and the son and daughter-in-law of local ranch owner Carol Duffy had taken Chase's eighteen-month-old sister.

Chase's age had been the stumbling block in finding him a home and with no openings in any foster homes, as a last resort, they'd placed him in the boarding school for boys in trouble just outside of town.

A year after the adoptions, the Brunos had left North-bridge, and the Reverend had no idea what had become of them.

Two years later, Carol Duffy's son and daughter-in-law had moved to Billings. Carol had died recently, and the Reverend guessed that there was a good chance that Carol's only granddaughter—Chase's sister—had inherited the ranch. The ranch was now up for sale through the town Realtor, who might be able to put Chase in touch with his sister.

As had been the case on the drive home from Billings the day before, Chase had been quiet and withdrawn after today's visit with the Reverend, and Hadley thought that his offer to shop for groceries and cook dinner tonight had been an excuse for him to get away for a little while, to be alone with his thoughts. So she'd agreed yet again to give Cody his bath and get him ready for bed on her own.

"Want to say good-night?" she asked Chase then, bringing Cody nearer.

"'Night," Chase said perfunctorily to Cody before focusing on the griddle in front of him again.

Cody ignored Chase completely, more interested in plucking at one of the small hoop earrings Hadley had put on today in an attempt to dress up the gray pants and camp shirt she was wearing.

"Can you say good-night, Cody?" she encouraged the baby.

"Oose," he said instead.

"Moose is already waiting for you in bed," she informed the infant. "Tell Chase night-night and you can go to Moose."

Cody merely went on playing with her earring and repeated, "Oose."

"I'm about ready to plate this," Chase informed her of the food he was preparing.

Hadley shook her head, wondering if there was ever going to be any bonding between these two.

Not tonight, she thought. And giving in to that fact,

she took Cody to the bedroom and tucked him into the crib, getting a nigh-nigh out of him when she said goodnight and kissed him on the forehead.

Returning to the open area of the loft, Hadley debated about telling Chase he needed to put more effort into making a connection with his nephew. But his back was to her and his broad shoulders were impressive in the pale blue shirt he wore, and his derriere looked oh-so-good in a pair of dark jeans, and somehow berating him just wasn't what she was in the mood for.

Besides, he'd had an emotionally difficult couple of days, she told herself. She didn't need to add to them.

So rather than scolding him, she joined him in the kitchen and said, "Is there anything I can do?"

"Pour wine. Otherwise we're all set—I even cleared some space on the dining table."

"Maybe after we eat we could do some organizing, move the furniture, start making this place look as if you really are living here now," Hadley suggested as she took the open bottle of wine to the table and poured it into the glasses. The two place settings were surrounded by boxes, Chase's laptop and other just-moved-in backlog.

"Maybe tomorrow," he said when he joined her, nixing that idea. Putting two full plates on the table, he explained their meal. "This is called The Rocky Mountain—probably because it's too much of a mishmash of things to be called anything else. It's eggs and potatoes and onions and peppers and sausage and mushrooms and olives and chunks of three different cheeses, and it's smothered in a green chili sauce that's a little spicy."

"Sounds great," she said as they sat down. "And it looks like a rocky mountain—I'll never be able to eat that much," she warned of the mound of food on the dish before her.

"Eat what you can. I'd be surprised if you could finish it all."

It was great, though, and she told him so after her first bite. And while she was curious about where he'd learned to cook and who had called that particular dish The Rocky Mountain, she was also slightly concerned about him. Concern won out over curiosity and thinking that it might be good for him to talk, she opted for trying to get him to open up about something weightier than food.

"I had the feeling that you might not have agreed with the Reverend today when he said going to the Priticks' after five years at the boys' home was a case of better-late-than-never. Was I wrong?"

Chase had just taken a bite of his food so he couldn't answer immediately and while she waited, Hadley wondered if he was going to talk to her about this or if he would nix that, too.

"Alma Pritick was a saint," he said without reservation. "No one could have been nicer to me than she was. And it was such a relief, after all the fear and uncertainty I had in the boys' home."

"But you weren't alone with Alma. There was her husband too… Homer…"

"Right—Homer," Chase said darkly. "And the only reason he agreed to take on a foster kid was for the stipend the state paid and for help around his farm. That was why they never adopted me—there was no way he was giving up the stipend and taking me on as his own kid."

"I don't really remember Alma Pritick…"

"Alma died when I was twelve," Chase said as if he still felt some sorrow. "Logan and I were friends even then, but before Alma died she made things more… homey…for me, so I didn't hang out at your house as much."

"But you only had four years with her?"

"Right. But during those four years, she was so good to me…"

Chase took a drink of his wine and stared for a moment into the glass as if he were remembering his late foster mother.

Then he said, "I think I probably filled a void for Alma the way she filled one for me. Homer would come in from the fields after work, not say a word to either of us, take his plate of food, walk into the living room with it and sit in front of the television until he went to bed. Literally days would go by without him speaking to her or even answering her if she spoke to him. So she would talk to me—she was the first person to actually say anything about my parents' deaths—"

"But she didn't tell you about your brothers and sisters?"

He shook his head. "Not a word. She was only interested in making me feel better, in convincing me that my folks loved me. She probably figured that talking about lost brothers and sisters would have made me unhappy, and she would never have done anything that might have caused that."

"That makes sense," Hadley agreed.

"Besides, Alma tried to keep things between us cheery—as much for her own benefit as mine, I think. I never understood how she could stand the life she had with Homer—the silence, the gruffness when he did speak to her, the total lack of regard or affection or even kindness. When she died, he didn't shed a tear. He went to the funeral, came home, changed into his overalls and went back to work as if nothing had changed."

"I never had the feeling that he was abusive to you. Was I wrong?" Hadley asked, fearing what the answer might be.

"As in beating me, or worse?" Chase shook his head. "No. Homer didn't even speak to me—other than to tell me what my chores were for the day or yelling if I didn't do something the way he wanted it done."

"And when Alma died there was just you and Homer..." Hadley said, delving a little deeper as she reached her fill of the meal he'd prepared and just sipped her wine.

"Yes," Chase confirmed with disgust.

"That couldn't have been good."

"The best I can say is that I still had a room to sleep in, food to eat, new work boots for birthdays and two shirts for Christmas—so I had something to wear when I washed the other one. There was no conversation, no how-was-your-day, nothing. If I got sick, I went to the school nurse. Every couple of years Homer took me to a dentist. When I hit teenage years he said one wrong move and I was out—and I knew he meant it."

"Wow, I guess that's one way to control a teenager."

"The day I graduated from high school, I went back to the farm after the ceremony, packed my duffel bag and found him out in the field. I said I was leaving. He said okay. And that was the extent of it—pretty much the way things had always been between Homer and me. I've never had contact with him since."

But there were some residual feelings, because when Chase pushed away his empty plate Hadley thought she saw anger in the shove.

"No wonder you spent so much time at our house," she said.

"Your stepmother might have been a pain in the neck, but after Alma died, your house was the only place I had any sense of family life. And it was the only place I could get a meal I didn't have to fix myself."

"I know Logan always said Homer Pritick was a jerk, that he wasn't nice to you. But I guess I didn't have any idea how things really were for you at home," Hadley said, realizing that her fantasy of Chase had been just that, that she hadn't really known him at all or anything about what he'd gone through.

"So," she said, thinking out loud, "connecting with people must have gotten to seem like you were asking to be hurt and maybe that's why you sort of keep yourself from connecting with Cody..."

Chase frowned at her and said defensively, "You think I'm not connecting with the kid?"

"Do you think you are connecting with Cody?"

Chase seemed to give that some consideration and when he spoke again the defensiveness was replaced by a reluctant concession. "I guess not."

Hadley thought it might be best to leave it at that, to let Chase think about things and make up his own mind about what sort of relationship he wanted to have with his nephew.

So she stood and began to clear their dinner dishes, saying as she did, "Where did you learn to make The Rocky Mountain?"

Chase stood, too, taking their wine glasses and following her into the kitchen area. "Logan and I worked as short-order cooks in a Colorado diner. It was their specialty."

"I didn't know you guys worked in a diner—does that mean you can cook more than this?"

"I can sling hash and burgers, cook an egg just about any way you want it and deep-fry everything. Logan can, too—you didn't know that?"

"I know he puts an equal effort into fixing meals around here. What else don't I know about the two of you?" she asked as she rinsed the plates.

"I don't know what you do know," Chase said reasonably.

"I know that you guys left the day after you graduated high school to have an adventure and travel the country. I know you were working somewhere different, doing something different—seeing someone different—every time I heard from Logan. But when it comes to particulars or what went on between the calls…"

"We did get around and do a lot of stuff," Chase confirmed. "We lived in more than half the states in the country and we worked at anything—and everything—that would give us money to live and travel to the next place."

"I've never been too clear about how you guys went from that to designing and making furniture—Logan didn't show any interest in anything artistic before he left home."

"That came out of our working in the furniture factories in North Carolina. I can't explain why, but for some reason, of all the jobs we'd had, that job just struck a note with both of us."

"Factory work?"

"No, not the factory work part of it, but the actual furniture making. We started talking about how pieces would look better and be more comfortable, how we'd improve them."

"And two stars of the furniture industry were born," Hadley joked as she closed the dishwasher, dried her hands and turned to lean against the counter and look at Chase.

He offered her a chocolate mint. After popping one into his mouth himself, he took up the same position against the island directly across from her, his hands grasping the counter's edge near his hips.

As chocolate melted to a minty delight in her mouth, she realized her line of vision went from one hand, across his zipper, to his other hand and yanked her eyes away in a hurry.

"By then I'd gone from Milan to Paris," Hadley said, thinking that it was slightly easier to overlook Chase's inherent sexiness when Cody was with them. But when she was alone with Chase, it seeped in and she just couldn't seem to overlook it…

Finish what you were saying so he doesn't know! she ordered herself.

"When I went to Europe," she continued, "Logan and I lost touch. So it seemed like one minute you guys were in North Carolina, the next minute you were Mackey and McKendrick Furniture Designs in New York, and then Logan was opening another workshop and show-room in Connecticut to be near Helene after they got married."

"The timetable was a lot longer than one minute to the next." Chase said with a laugh. "For almost two years Mackey and McKendrick Furniture Designs was just what we put on the business cards that made it look like we knew what we were doing. The truth was, between whatever work we could pick up to pay for rent, food and supplies, we were making armchairs in the middle of a studio apartment the size of Cody's bedroom and lugging the chairs ourselves through the streets of New York to deliver them."

"So how did you go from that to where you are now?" Hadley asked.

"We finally found a couple of decorators who liked our stuff and either bought some pieces for their clients or used us in showcases that got us some exposure. It built up from there, but it was much slower going than you're making it out to be."

"And now the two of you are the It Men when it comes to furniture as art."

Chase laughed and flinched. "The It Men? I don't even know what that means."

"I admire your modesty, but you know you guys have done well for yourselves."

"We don't have any complaints," he said with a smile she sort of got stuck on.

A smile that was warm and endearing, that showed his straight white teeth and drew creases at the corners of those sky-blue eyes. A smile that had her thinking about how supple his lips were, about that kiss they'd shared the night before—that kiss she'd tried so hard not to think about all day and all evening because thinking about it made her want another one so much she could hardly see straight.

Then Chase said, "This is something new for me tonight."

This time she was afraid her drifting off had caused her to miss something.

Baffled and hoping she wasn't giving herself away, she said, "What's new for you?"

"Talking like this with a woman. I tend to keep things strictly light and airy with women."

"Of course you do," Hadley said. Her words came out with a hint of flirtatiousness that she regretted.

Still, something about it made him laugh. And his laugh was even better than his smile.

"You didn't even know where your own brother learned to cook, don't try to tell me you know anything about how I am with women."

"Light and airy?" Hadley ventured.

He laughed again. "I'm just saying that it's usually Logan I talk to—particularly about the serious stuff. But tonight I've been talking to you the way I talk to him, and that's a new experience for me."

"Maybe you just see me as my brother's stand-in," she said, not particularly pleased with that possibility.

"Or maybe you're just easy to talk to," he said in a tone that had gone softer.

Easy to talk to because I'm as familiar and comfortable as an old shoe?

"I guess that's a good thing…" she said unenthusiastically. "I should probably head for home."

Chase didn't comment on that as he stood there, looking at her intently, almost as if he were seeing something in her that he hadn't seen before. And maybe liking it?

Then Chase pushed off the counter's edge and closed the space that separated them. His hands came to cup both sides of her face, to tilt it upward as his mouth lowered to hers. Taking it. Taking control of it in a kiss that held nothing back right from the start.

She let her lips part in response to his. She closed her eyes and raised her hands to the solid wall of his chest, reveling in the feel of it.

Chase's lips parted further and she followed his lead.

His fingers delved into her hair, his thumbs caressed her temples and her palms pressed more firmly to his pectorals as she did a little massaging of her own.

And when there was movement and sway to that kiss, Hadley was right there with him, moving, swaying, kissing him every bit as soundly as he was kissing her, and not surprised when his tongue joined the party.

That was new and nice, and the added intimacy sent a wave of something all glittery and tingly through her.

He wrapped his arms around her then, pulling her closer, making that kiss more powerful. They were wiping the slate clean of anything that had ever existed in the past—real or imagined—and opening up an entirely different playing field between them. A playing field on which neither of them held more ground than the other.

A playing field on which Hadley wasn't alone in her attraction to Chase. On which she began to believe the feeling was mutual.

That was a heady thought and it somehow translated into the kiss becoming more intense, running away with both of them.

And maybe that was why Hadley knew it had to end there. Before it actually did run away with them both.

She applied just enough pressure to Chase's chest to let him know they needed to slow this down, to stop it.

He slowed it down, but it was clear he wasn't eager to stop it. He took a little time with that—not abandoning her tongue too quickly, lingering a moment longer before he finally quit, came back and then quit again.

But he didn't let go of her. He kept hold of her, changing only his posture so he could rest the underside of his chin to the top of her head.

"You have to tell me not to do that," he said in a raspy voice. "Maybe if you do I'll be able not to."

"Don't do that?" she said, making it a question rather than a command and saying it without any conviction at all.

Chase laughed. "I don't think that'll work."

Good...

But in spite of the way she felt, she knew this couldn't

continue. So she found the willpower to lean as far back as she could, peer up at that handsome face and say with more strength than she thought she had, "We're going to be working together, living here together. There's Logan. And—"

"Too many complications," Chase finished as if she were saying exactly what he was thinking.

"Waa-ay too many complications," she confirmed.

But something about their exchange only made him smile mischievously, as if he were looking at this as a challenge.

"Seriously," she said. "Behave yourself."

He stepped back, letting go of her in the process and holding up his hands—palms out—as if in surrender. "Behaving," he swore. "From here on. I know I have to."

"It's for the best," she said, telling herself that it really was even though it was difficult for her to actually believe.

Then she said, "Now I really do need to get going."

Chase didn't walk her to the door. Whatever his reasons were, she thought it was better that he didn't, that a good-night there might lead to another kiss that shouldn't happen.

But as she left, Chase's voice came from the kitchen area, not sounding as if he'd turned toward her.

"That time you spent in Paris?" he said.

"Yeah…" she answered, not turning either.

"It was worth it. Because the French kissing? Best ever…"

Hadley couldn't help grinning.

But she didn't say anything.

She just left the loft and closed the door behind her.

Chapter Seven

One of the things Chase would need to do now that he was living in a country setting rather than in the city was buy himself a car. But until he could he had access to Logan's SUV. As he backed it out of the garage late on Thursday afternoon, he took a last look at Hadley. She was standing where he'd left her—at the foot of the steps to her apartment over the garage—holding Cody and trying to get the baby to wave to him.

But it wasn't the sight of the baby that he couldn't get enough of. It was Hadley.

Her hair gleamed in the September sunshine. Her skin was like alabaster. She was cute and beautiful at the same time. Along with being sweet and funny and smart and warm and kind, easy to talk to and sympathetic.

And when he'd left her a few minutes before, he'd damn near kissed her goodbye as if he had the right to...

Chase returned Hadley's wave and backed the remainder of the way down the drive, thinking about her.

Thinking about her the way he was always thinking about her these days. And nights.

Hadley was great. He loved every minute he was with her. And he couldn't wait to be with her again from the moment they parted company to the first chance he had to set eyes on her again.

Plus there was the kissing.

It all added up to something he recognized too well, something he knew shouldn't be going on, feelings he shouldn't be having.

And the feelings were powerhouse.

This was not supposed to be happening with his best friend and business partner's little sister. This was not supposed to happen with someone he was about to work with. This was a very dangerous mixing of the long-term and the short-term.

So he should just stop, he told himself as he headed in the direction of Homer Pritick's farm.

But he wasn't exactly sure what he should stop.

The kissing, for sure.

But the rest?

The rest didn't mean what it had always meant with other women. It didn't mean meeting a woman he found attractive, flirting with her, exercising the seduction muscles, wooing her into bed and maybe into a relationship that would last as long as the fun did.

Things just weren't the same with Hadley.

Sure, he was attracted to her—like gangbusters! He couldn't get the image of her out of his head; he actually felt a need to be with her every minute, he wanted to touch her so badly, he ached. Sometimes he was even ridiculously jealous of the attention she paid Cody.

But on top of all that, he could talk to her as easily as he talked to Logan. He was every bit as relaxed, as at home, with Hadley as he was with her brother. More, even, than he was with Logan in some ways, since he'd never told Logan about being scared at the boys' home or anything about the way things had been for him when Alma Pritick was alive. He hadn't been as open about his feelings.

So it wasn't as if what was going on with Hadley came out of the fact that she was Logan's sister, or that he knew Hadley from childhood. This was something else that he couldn't quite put his finger on. It was different from any relationship he'd ever had with a woman, too.

But he shouldn't even be thinking this way. The fact was that getting into anything romantic with Hadley could lead to problems when the romance ended.

Unless…

What if a little post-divorce fling was all Hadley was interested in? Something that would boost her confidence? Something that would get her back in the game? A palate cleanser?

He didn't know anything about her marriage or her divorce. Logan had been sketchy about the details. He had told him Hadley had met someone and was going to marry him. Chase had said, that's nice. End of conversation. A few years later Logan had said his sister was getting divorced. Chase had said, too bad. End of conversation.

So Chase didn't have any idea what had gone on with Hadley, but having suffered through a divorce might have some bearing on her own view of relationships.

As he turned onto the road that led to Homer Pritick's house, he decided that he needed to feel Hadley out about her marriage's breakup and how she saw things since then.

And he needed to let her know where he stood when it came to relationships.

If the fiasco of his last relationship had taught him anything, it was that he had to make sure his own views on these things were perfectly clear. And that he had better do some delving into the woman's viewpoint, too, before anything went any further.

So that's what he was going to do.

At least for starters. Because there was no harm in it.

And maybe when they both knew where they stood, that alone would be enough to cool things. Hell, it had happened before—there had been any number of women who had heard his stance on relationships and said *no thanks.*

But maybe he and Hadley were on the same page with this stuff. And if they were on the same page? a little voice of reason in the back of his mind asked.

Well, then he guessed he'd go from there....

As long as it didn't mean doing anything to hurt her....

But for the moment he was on Pritick property and he had something else he had to do, something else he had to think about. So as he turned off his engine he put thoughts of Hadley on hold.

He got out of the SUV and looked up at the house that had never been a home to him.

It was just as it had always been before—the two-story farmhouse was whitewashed and impeccably maintained without any sign of warmth or welcome.

Chase didn't bother going up to the front door. He'd timed his visit knowing that this was when Homer would come in from working the fields, when he would be picking the day's ripe vegetables from his garden.

The garden was behind the house so that was where Chase went, stopping just as he rounded the corner in order to give himself a moment to take in his first sight in seventeen years of his former foster father.

Homer had aged but even hunkered down pulling tomatoes off their vines Chase could tell that he was still all solid, stocky farmer in his denim overalls and faded plaid shirt. His black hair had grayed and thinned, and his suntanned skin looked more like old leather than it had before, but of the wrinkles that marked it there were no laugh lines.

After he'd made the decision to move back to Northbridge, Chase had debated about whether or not he would ever come out here and pay any kind of visit to Homer. He hadn't been inclined to and had thought it more likely that they would merely encounter each other on Main Street at some point, that they would nod, maybe not speak or speak very little and go on again as if they hadn't shared the same house for ten years.

That would have suited Chase just fine.

But for no reason he could explain, this morning he'd recalled that when he'd come from the boys' home to live with the Priticks he'd had a small suitcase. And that recollection had made him wonder if that small suitcase had been kept, and what might be in it if it had been, if there might be something in it about his brothers and sisters.

And the only way to find that out was to visit Homer and ask.

So here he was.

Go on, get it over with, he advised himself as he stood at the corner of the house and watched the farmer use a pocketknife to dig a weed out from between two cucumber plants and toss it to the outskirts of the garden.

He wasn't afraid to come face-to-face with Homer again. But it wasn't something he was looking forward to, either. It just was what it was. He didn't expect any kind of warm welcome; he didn't expect Homer to be happy to see him. He didn't expect anything, really. And that was what he got when Homer stood up and caught sight of him.

After a moment of the older man staring at him expressionlessly, the guttural voice that Chase had heard so infrequently growing up boomed across the yard, reminding Chase of one of the many reasons he'd never liked Homer Pritick.

"Well, if it isn't the mutt..."

Thursday night marked the beginning of the high school's Homecoming weekend. To kick off the festivities there was a huge bonfire being lit on the outskirts of town to fire up the team. Even though it was a little late for Cody, Chase had suggested that he, Hadley and Cody go in order to get into the spirit of things since they had plans to attend Friday night's game, as well.

Hadley hadn't been too sure he would still be in the mood for the bonfire after seeing Homer Pritick. But unlike the occasions on which they'd attempted to do some fact-finding about Chase's history and about his brothers and sisters, Chase seemed undisturbed by his visit to his former foster father.

So at eight o'clock that night, Hadley, Chase and Cody were in the midst of the loud revelry of a small-town turnout—band music, cheerleaders doing cheers and the general spectacle that went with showing the high-school team that everyone was rooting for them.

The open field was too rocky to allow for Cody's stroller. After seeing what other dads of infants were doing, Chase coaxed Cody to go to him and lifted the baby to straddle his neck, keeping hold of Cody's hands to secure him.

Hadley was surprised that it didn't frighten the child. Cody seemed to find everything around them fascinating from his high perch.

Once the cheers were over and the bonfire lit, there was popped kettle corn and other goodies provided by the Booster Club. The hot apple cider chased away the chill that came with a September night that warned that autumn was on its way. That was when the crowd began to mingle as if it were a party.

"Is that you, Chase Mackey?" a woman with ample cleavage, bright eyes and a come-hither smile meant for Chase alone approached them and demanded. "I can't believe what I'm seeing! Could it really be Mr. I'll-Never-Ever-Get-Married with a wife and a baby? I heard you were moving back to town but nobody said anything about a family."

Chase laughed. "Lydia Thatcher." He returned the greeting with a name that was only vaguely familiar to Hadley. "Yeah, it's me," he went on to say. "But I hate to bust your bubble—this is Hadley McKendrick, Logan McKendrick's little sister, not my wife. And this guy up top is my nephew—that's as close to family as I've gotten so far."

"How could you have a nephew when you didn't have brothers or sisters?" the other woman challenged.

"Long story," Chase said, not telling it. "How are you doin'?"

"Better than ever and I won't let anyone say different," the woman answered, flirting outrageously. "I'm single and available and having the time of my life!"

"I'll bet you are," Chase said with another laugh while Hadley tried to place the woman.

Hadley's early crush on Chase had made it difficult for her to think of him with other girls. Of course she'd been aware that he had a bevy of girlfriends, but she'd tried to block it out as much as possible.

Now she was reasonably sure that Lydia Thatcher had been one of those girlfriends for a while. That must be why she recognized the name, even though she didn't recognize the other woman.

But as for resenting her still? That was another story.

Or maybe Hadley just didn't appreciate that the other woman hadn't so much as spared her a glance or said hello or acknowledged her existence once Lydia had found out that Hadley was not Chase's wife. And the fact that Lydia Thatcher was openly coming on to Chase as if Hadley wasn't there at all didn't help matters, even though Hadley told herself that she shouldn't care. Chase was a free agent, there was nothing but a renewed friendship between them—French kissing or not—and what he did with other women or what other women did with him wasn't any of her business.

Regardless of what she told herself, Hadley was actually entertaining a daydream of pretending to trip and pour cider down Lydia's cleavage.

To Chase's credit, he was friendly to the other woman without flirting back or encouraging her, and at the first opportunity he said, "It's nice to see you, Lydia, but I promised Hadley one of those brownies over there before we take Cody home, and it looks like they're going fast."

Hadley had mentioned that she would rather have a brownie than a caramel apple but the only promise Chase had made to her tonight was to try to give Cody a bath and put the baby to bed without her assistance.

She wasn't about to correct him and stall the escape Chase was providing for them, though, so she kept that information to herself.

"You should have my cell-phone number," Lydia insisted rather than letting them go too easily.

"It's a small town—I'm sure I can get it," Chase said. "Good to see you, though," he reiterated, turning to Hadley and nodding with his oh-so-sexily-dented chin for Hadley to go in the direction of the table where treats were being served.

Barely out of earshot of Lydia, Chase leaned close to Hadley and said, "What do you say to getting the brownies to go? After I try my hand at the bath and bedtime stuff with Cody tonight, we can build our own fire and eat our brownies then?"

And you'll save Lydia Thatcher for a later date? Hadley was tempted to ask.

But she didn't. Instead she agreed as they reached the snack table, snatched two of the brownies that were precut and wrapped in plastic wrap, and then followed Chase to Logan's SUV.

Hadley was tempted to talk about Chase's past with Lydia Thatcher on the way home, but before she'd broached the subject, Chase said, "You never asked how it went with Homer this afternoon."

He was right, she hadn't. Purposely.

"I didn't want to pry," she said. "But since you brought it up...how did it go?"

Chase shrugged. "He hasn't changed. I'm still the mutt and he's still a stone wall."

"The mutt?" Hadley repeated.

"That's what he always called me—he said I was like a stray dog Alma had made him take in. A mutt."

"That's awful!"

Chase shrugged again.

"And he called you that today?"

"It was the first thing he said to me. Nice guy, that Homer," Chase added sarcastically.

"Did he have anything else to say?"

A third shrug. "It was the way I thought it would be. I asked if he knew anything about my having brothers and sisters. He did, but he didn't think it was important enough to pay any attention to. He had no idea what happened to them. And couldn't have cared less."

"And were you remembering right? Was there a suitcase?"

"There was. But Homer threw it out a long time ago. Since there was nothing in it but the clothes I'd come to them with, he didn't see any reason to keep it."

"Just clothes? No toys or blankets or anything that might have been important to you?"

"Like a moose?" he joked.

"Oose?" Cody said from the backseat.

"Like a moose," Hadley confirmed, reaching into the backseat to show Cody that his moose was alongside him in his car seat. "Or any pictures or mementos or anything?"

"Just clothes," Chase repeated. "Alma found a picture of my folks in an old newspaper—she framed it and I still have it. But otherwise I apparently came with pretty much nothing."

"That's awful," she said.

Chase shrugged yet again. "I don't think I'm any the worse for wear for it."

"I don't care, this is just breaking my heart…"

Chase looked away from his driving again to grin at her. "That's the last thing I want to do," he said. "So let's talk about something cheerier."

Hadley was lost in picturing him as a little boy, but Chase took care of finding a cheerier subject himself. "After talking to Homer I went by the Realtor's office."

"Are you moving before your boxes are even unpacked?" she asked, making a feeble joke.

"I went to ask about the Duffy ranch—remember yesterday the Rev said—"

"The Reverend would hate it if he heard you call him that," Hadley said, still putting effort into anything that would lighten the tone.

"Wouldn't he?" Chase agreed as if that thought delighted him. Then he went on. "Remember that the Rev said he thought my younger sister could have inherited that farm? Well, he was right. Her name is Shannon Duffy—apparently when she was adopted, the parents kept the name that Angie knew her by. It was on the DVD. Anyway, she did inherit the farm and she is selling it."

"Did you tell the Realtor your family history so she would put the two of you in contact?" Hadley asked.

"I just hit the high points for the Realtor without going into too much. But I did get Shannon Duffy's phone number out of it—and she does still live in Billings."

"That's kind of exciting," Hadley said, seizing on the positive as they pulled onto the drive that led around to the garage and her apartment. "Did you call the number?"

"No. I need to think about what I'm going to say to her before I make that call."

Chase pulled into the garage, turned off the engine and they both got out of the SUV.

Hadley wasn't sure if Chase would get Cody out of the car seat so she opened the back door on her side. But then he leaped in to unbuckle the safety seat's belts and take Cody out while Hadley merely grabbed the diaper bag.

"Come on, big guy, to the tub," Chase said, seeming to put an end to their conversation.

Hadley met them at the garage door. In keeping with the change of topic, she leaned toward man and baby to say to Cody, "Tonight you really rate, Cody. Your uncle passed on Lydia Thatcher just to give you a bath."

"That's what she thinks," Chase confided to the infant as they headed for Chase's loft next door. "No offense, Code-man, but I passed on Lydia Thatcher to eat brownies with this one just as soon as I can clean you up and get you to bed...."

Chapter Eight

"Better?" Hadley asked, barely suppressing a laugh at Chase as he came out of his bedroom about an hour after they'd left the Homecoming bonfire.

"The kid must hate me," Chase grumbled.

"Cody doesn't hate you," Hadley said.

Once they'd returned to the loft, Hadley had given Chase plenty of safety warnings, made sure the water was the right temperature and offered a lengthy explanation of how to give an almost-one-year-old a bath. Then she'd left Chase in charge and gone into the nursery to set out Cody's diaper and pajamas.

The bathroom door had been ajar just in case, and Chase had done a play-by-play commentary of his actions to reassure her that all was well.

And all had been well.

Until Chase had said, "Okay, I think we're done, I'm going to take him out now..."

And that was when the exclamations—and expletives—had sent Hadley running into the bathroom.

The problem had occurred as Chase had lifted the wet, naked baby out of the tub.

And Cody had baptized his uncle in a happy little stream of urine.

After Chase's total freak-out, Hadley had taken over with Cody while Chase had charged out of the bathroom in horror, leaving a laughing Hadley to put Cody to bed and clean up.

Now here Chase was, his hair just beginning to dry from a shampooing, his skin rosy from what must have been quite a scrubbing. He was wearing clean jeans and buttoning a chambray shirt he'd left untucked so the tails hung free around his hips.

Hadley forced herself not to stare too long at the strip of chest that was only visible for a moment before he finished fastening the buttons.

"You don't do that to somebody you like!"

Hadley's mouth had gone a little dry but still she said, "Remember when I warned you about changing a baby boy's diaper? Well, the same thing happens with them when they have baths. It isn't personal."

"The kid whizzed on me!"

Hadley laughed. "He only whizzes on the ones he loves?" she suggested, trying a different tack. Then she added, "Think of it this way, maybe it's a sign that he's feeling more comfortable with you, that he isn't tense, that he can just let go…"

"You're enjoying this waa-ay too much."

"I really am," she said, unable to keep from laughing any longer.

She was also enjoying the sight of him rolling his sleeves to his elbows. But she thought that he was too enmeshed in his revulsion to notice.

"I'm heating the brownies—I like them warm," she informed him then, trying to move on.

"I'll pour the port, but at this point I'm wishing it was something a whole lot stronger," Chase said, going to the packing box he'd found when they'd first come home and taking out a bottle of the dessert wine he'd assured her would be perfect with the brownies.

"You can have something stronger if you want it. I'm fine with just the brownie," she said.

"No, I'll stick with the port," he said, still grumbling but not seriously now.

While Chase poured two glasses, Hadley took the brownies out of the oven and set them on plates. "Forks or fingers?" she asked.

"I'm good with fingers."

It was on the tip of Hadley's tongue to ask him exactly what he was good at with his fingers…

But she refrained, warning herself about where her mind kept going tonight. And to stop it!

There were no napkins, so Hadley tore off squares of

the paper towels she'd brought over earlier in the week. She took those and the brownies into the living-room section of the loft where Chase had started a fire in the fireplace before beginning Cody's bath.

She set Chase's brownie on the coffee table and sat down on the leather couch, facing the fire.

Chase joined her with the wine, sitting beside her— not too close but not too far away, either.

For no reason Hadley could fathom, she noticed then that he was in stocking feet. And between that and his just-thrown-on casual clothes, and the fact that he smelled of a heavenly soap, there was something about it all that made things seem more intimate.

"Brownies," he said as he broke off a corner of his using two of those fingers he claimed to be good with.

Hadley forced herself to think about the chocolate confection rather than Chase.

"Do we know who made them?" he asked.

Brownies…brownies…he's talking about brownies…

"All I know is that they're dark, fudgy, they have crispy, crackly tops and inside there are little pockets of melted chocolate chunks," Hadley rhapsodized to conceal the fact that her mind kept wandering to him. But it was actually lucky that there was something decadently chocolate to distract her. And to help soothe the things he was stirring in her tonight.

She took her second bite and sighed in chocolate

bliss. Or maybe in resignation that the brownie was all she could have…

"I'm getting the idea that you're a fan of chocolate," Chase said, interpreting the sigh as he took a second bite of his. "But you're right—these are terrific. Maybe we should have swiped a couple of extras."

"Then I would have eaten them all…" Out of sexual frustration if nothing else…

The port did go well with the brownies. Chase told her about another raspberry wine that she should also try someday. That gave Hadley something concrete to concentrate on while they finished eating.

Then it was only the wine and the fire they were left with and she was right back to thinking about Chase and the way his jeans hinted at muscular thighs so close beside hers on the couch…

After setting his empty plate on the coffee table, Chase sat back again in a way that angled him more toward Hadley than the fire. He stretched an arm along the back of the sofa, looked more fixedly at her, and said, "So, Lydia Thatcher—sorry about her. She was rude to not even say hello to you."

Another subject. Hadley was glad he'd introduced it, because she was still having trouble thinking about anything but him.

"Lydia Thatcher is one of your old girlfriends, isn't she?" Hadley asked as if it wasn't something she'd kept track of.

"An old *crazy* girlfriend," he said with no affection

whatsoever. "I went out with her for three weeks senior year and she started hounding me with the bizarre idea of how romantic it would be if we ran off and got married the way she'd seen in some movie."

"And your answer must have been that you were never—ever—going to get married?" Hadley said, referring to the other woman's Mr. I'll-Never-Ever-Get-Married greeting.

"That was my answer and the end of dating Lydia Thatcher."

"And is that what's gone on from there? When the woman you're involved with wants marriage, you end it?"

"Oh, no," he said emphatically. "I don't lead anybody on—it just cost me a whole lot of money to prove that in court."

Logan had told Hadley that Chase had hit a bump in the road when it came to women, that that had been a contributing factor in their decision to return to North-bridge. That's all her brother had said and he definitely hadn't mentioned anything about a legal matter. Hadley had assumed Chase had been caught in a compromising position or something...

"You've lost me," Hadley said. "You just proved in a court of law that you don't lead women on?"

"I had to. The last woman I was involved with sued me for breach of promise."

Hadley knew her eyes had gone to saucer-size but she couldn't help it. "You're kidding?"

"I wish I was."

"What did you promise her?" Hadley asked.

"That's just it, I didn't promise her anything. Her or anyone else. In fact, the opposite is true—I'm always up front with any woman I get involved with about what I think of marriage. And what I think of marriage is that it's not for me—"

"Because you've always had too much fun playing around," Hadley said.

Chase smiled. "Logan did some reporting?"

"He didn't have to report when you guys lived here—there weren't many girls in your high-school class who you didn't date. And Logan said that since then, you've been bouncing from one woman to the next like a pinball."

"I have enjoyed the company of my fair share of women, yes," Chase acknowledged.

"But never without letting them know that marriage is not in the cards," Hadley finished for him. "And why is that?"

"Why isn't marriage an option? I just don't think it works," he said simply enough.

"There are plenty of good marriages," Hadley contended.

"Are we talking good or just unbroken? Because the fact that people don't get divorced doesn't necessarily make it a good marriage."

"I'm talking good—as in two people who like each

other and love each other and enjoy being with each other—there are marriages like that."

"Maybe," he said as if he still didn't agree. "But even in those it seems to me that people are just settling. Lowering their expectations."

"That's not true!"

"All I know is that from what I've seen, when the bloom is off, when things aren't so exciting and thrilling and fun, then it's the flaws that take center stage. Then I'm not thinking that you have the most beautiful eyes I've ever seen, I'm thinking why do you have to talk to me during the most crucial part of the football game. Then I'm not thinking that I love to make you smile, I'm thinking why do I have to take out the trash right this minute. Then I'm not thinking that I might go out of my mind if I can't kiss you or touch you, I'm thinking why did you leave your razor on the shower floor for me to step on…"

"So there's no taking the bad with the good with you? It's either all fun and games or you want out?"

He grinned as if he were getting a kick out of debating this with her. "On top of the Priticks, I also saw your stepmother and how much she rode roughshod over your dad—you know it probably didn't start out that way. But it ended up with your dad spending almost all his home time in the garage to avoid her. Did you see that as the way either of them should have spent the biggest part of their lives?"

"No, but—"

"Isn't it conceivable that they both could have just had the good part at the beginning and when that was over, skipped the rest?"

"That would have been better for Logan and me, but then there wouldn't have been my half brothers and sisters. Tessa, Issa, Zeli, Tucker and Dag are great additions to the world."

"But we aren't talking kids now, or populating the world. We're talking relationships, marriage—"

"And the warped way you view them."

Chase laughed. "Not warped. Realistic. There were plenty of other marriages I saw as a kid that didn't have anything to recommend them, that were just people trudging through their lives, sticking with what they'd gotten themselves into without being happy. Then I grew up and saw the marriages of people my own age. I watched them go downhill from where they began. Logan's first marriage turned sour and ended in divorce. Yours apparently went south somehow or you wouldn't be divorced…"

Her own marriage had definitely gone south and couldn't be used to support her side of this, so she offered nothing on that score.

"I'm just saying," Chase continued, "that I don't want to have to use divorce as the end to relationships. I like to have the good part of the relationship, to enjoy it. And when that relationship changes and stops being fun, I can say goodbye without the need for lawyers and courts and hard feelings, and just move on. Or at least that's what I aim for—my last one blew that…"

"Not everything about a lasting relationship changes for the worst," Hadley argued. "Sure, it mellows with age, but that can make it even better. Only you wouldn't know that because it sounds to me like the minute things get serious, you're out the door."

"Serious is okay. I can do serious. I was with Courtney for over a year."

"Courtney being the last woman you were with, the one who sued you for breach of promise?" Hadley asked.

"Courtney Waxell. Unfortunately of Waxell, Waxell and Waxell—Courtney, her father and her brother—all high-powered, high-profile attorneys who specialize in suing people."

"For breach of promise when some guy takes up a year of a woman's life in a relationship that even he admits was serious and then—for some reason—bails on?"

"Ouch! I'm glad they didn't talk to you!" Chase said, but he wasn't taking offense because he was smiling again. Hadley smiled back and tucked her feet up underneath her on the sofa.

"I let Courtney know from day one that marriage was not on the table," Chase said. "I've had reasonably long relationships with a lot of women who don't think that just because we went past the six-month mark I might marry them anyway."

"But apparently Courtney did."

"And luckily just thinking I might marry her is not the same as a promise to marry her."

"So you won the lawsuit?"

"I did. When a number of former girlfriends testified that it was my habit to make myself abundantly crystal clear when it came to marriage and how it's something I'm determined not to do. But the lawsuit went on longer than the relationship and cost me an arm and a leg."

"A number of former girlfriends," Hadley repeated.

"Like I said, I've enjoyed the company of my fair share of women."

"And is that how you see your whole life stretching out for you—just a string of women so long you won't even be able to remember them all? Never reaching any kind of deeper level with any one of them? Never really connecting to any one of them? Never really getting to know them enough to actually know them?"

"I think I do actually get to know them and they actually get to know me," he defended himself.

"Not well enough to keep quiet at some crucial sports moment, and pick up her razors from the shower floor," Hadley said with a laugh. "Not well enough to have something deeper and more meaningful with each other."

"Deep enough to know how not to annoy each other— but you're so miserable you want to? Or you can end up divorced and then you're exactly where I am, only you had to go through a divorce to get there."

"I never knew you were this cynical," Hadley accused.

"I don't think I am," Chase defended himself again. "I told you—I'm just realistic."

Hadley shook her head at him. "And I'll bet it just so happens that that realism also allows you to juggle more than one woman at once, too."

"That depends—are we talking about cheating? Because I can honestly say that that's something I haven't ever done—"

"Come on," Hadley said skeptically. "You don't expect me to believe that..."

"I have never cheated," he swore. "I've dated more than one woman at a time, but not without the women being aware that we weren't exclusive and knowing I was okay with them dating other guys, too. But for the most part, I'm all about concentrating on one woman. In fact, what got me into trouble with Courtney is that when I'm involved with someone, I'm a pretty devoted guy—Courtney took that as a promise."

"But you're only devoted until the thrill is gone, and then you devote yourself to someone else," Hadley said, raising an eyebrow at him.

He studied her for a moment, his expression unreadable, before he gave her a crooked smile and said, "You know, as much as I like debating you, I don't think I want to talk about other women with you."

He was looking very intently at her. Hadley met that

gaze and couldn't help goading him. "Because I won't let you slide."

He laughed. "Or maybe because other women are not what I want to talk about—or think about—when I'm with you."

"Oh, good one! I'll bet a lot of women fall for that line."

He laughed again. "I've never used it before but yeah, I thought it would work."

Hadley laughed, too. Then, in conclusion, she said, "Well, all I know is that light and breezy and carefree may be great for a while, but eventually I think you'll crave more substance."

His smile turned wicked and there was a sexy twinkle in his sky-blue eyes. "Craving something—that I'm already doing…" he said, smoothing her cheek with the backs of his fingers.

He went on studying her, searching her eyes as if something were to be found in them. Maybe something that would keep him at bay.

And Hadley knew there should have been something there to warn him away from what she sensed he was considering.

But looking into that marvelously masculine face, all she could think about was how much she wanted him to kiss her.

"God, I wish I knew what the rules were here…" Chase whispered more to himself than to her before he leaned forward and kissed the side of her neck.

She knew there were important reasons why she shouldn't do this.

But his breath was warm against her neck, the hand that had been on the top of the sofa moments before had found its way into her hair and his other hand had somehow gone from that feather stroke of her face to resting on her hip where it was doing a sensual massage through her jeans.

Plus he smelled like heaven, and oh, what the man could do as he nibbled his way to the hollow of her throat...

"Wasn't there some talk last night about behaving?" she asked feebly in a voice that was breathy and more of an invitation than anything else.

"There was," he confirmed, his own voice guttural and so sexy it stirred Hadley as much as the trail of kisses he was placing along her jawline. "I'll bet we were supposed to do it, weren't we? Behave?"

"I think so," she said, letting her head fall back to accommodate him.

"When should we start?" he asked.

"Soon?" she proposed just before his mouth covered hers in a soft, soft kiss. Just before she raised a hand to his nape.

"Soon," he assured between the end of that kiss and the even deeper one that followed.

But soon wasn't now, as they began the sequel to what had been initiated the previous night. Their mouths opened wider and his tongue didn't hesitate to invade. To play and lure and entice.

Hadley's hand went up the back of his head, testing the coarseness of his hair, maybe holding him to that kiss a little as she answered it with every bit as much fervor, as much enthusiasm, as much revelry.

He applied some pressure to her hip to move her nearer, to raise her onto his leg that was curved along the sofa cushion, leaving her sitting on his inner thigh.

So close…

She was so close to parts of his body that she shouldn't be that close to…

And that intimacy only turned her on all the more.

Her other arm went around him so she could lay her palm to his broad, hard back, grateful that the chambray of his shirt was as thin as it was and yet still wishing it wasn't there at all. Wishing her own tight U-necked T-shirt and the binding bra-strapped tank top underneath it weren't there to constrain her breasts, which suddenly seemed swollen with yearning. A yearning that was growing inside of her, taking over as his hand inched upward from her hip, slowly rising to the side of her rib cage.

He paused there and she very nearly groaned in complaint. But instead Hadley made their kiss more intense. It was Hadley's tongue that grew bolder, a silent message accentuated with a slight arch of her spine.

Chase answered it all with his mouth, his hand finally coming around to enclose her breast in a firm hold.

Massaging, kneading—it would have been wonderful if not for those two layers of knit fabric muting it.

Chase solved that problem, wasting little time before he slipped his hand under both of her shirts.

And then Hadley was grateful for the compression of the tight tank top, because it held his hand closer to her, aiding the cause of that big, slightly callused palm engulfing her naked flesh so her nipple could harden into it and beg for more.

She was putty in that hand as his fingers pressed into her, as he caressed and teased and tantalized…

And then abandoned her…

No, don't stop! she would have shrieked had he not had her mouth so busy.

But he used that hand to pull one of her legs around him, to maneuver her so that she was facing him more completely, straddling him.

When he had her where he wanted her, his hand found the hem of her shirts again, this time pulling them up high enough to leave her exposed.

For a brief moment Hadley looked at Chase. What she saw in his face told her he was as lost to desire as she was, as lost to what was drawing them together, despite everything that said they should resist it.

Then, as if he could do nothing to stop himself, he rediscovered one breast with his hand and the other with his mouth, and her head fell back as everything inside of her suddenly went into overdrive, wiping away all rational thought.

Her shoulders drew back, her spine arched and she lost herself in the feel of that mouth working wonders on her. Her hands were in his hair, they were running the width of his broad back, they were digging into biceps that could easily take the pressure. Her leg closed around behind him, reseating her even more securely to that part of him that let her know she wasn't the only one of them approaching the point of no return...

But she was approaching that point, and the evidence that he was, too, penetrated the yearning that was clouding her brain and gave her pause.

Where was this going?

Should she let it get there?

She wanted to...

She wanted him.

In the worst way...

But should she let herself have him?

She didn't know. And somehow her hesitation must have conveyed itself to him because as Hadley was trying to make a decision about whether or not to allow this to go any further, Chase rose up from her breast to kiss her again on the mouth—soundly, longingly, but with slightly more reserve as his hand took one parting caress of her other breast before he pulled her shirts down.

Then he kissed and nibbled his way to her ear where he whispered, "Back to behaving?"

Hadley couldn't keep the reluctant sigh from escaping her throat, but she didn't argue with him.

"Back to behaving," he concluded in a voice laden with disappointment.

Then he sat back enough to look into her eyes, to cup her face gently in both of his palms, holding it to kiss her again, softly but with feeling before he said, "We have a problem."

"I know," Hadley answered.

"I can't keep my hands off of you—"

"But there's Logan and work and—"

"Complications," he finished with what they'd decided at the end of the previous evening, too.

"Complications," Hadley confirmed, knowing that there were more of them for her than he realized because he and the way he lived his life—the way he intended to go on living it—were stumbling blocks for her. Huge stumbling blocks…

"But I can't keep my hands off of you," Chase repeated.

And the bigger problem was that she didn't want him to.

"I guess we better really, really think about this," he said.

His thumbs traced her cheekbones while he studied her as if he were memorizing every feature just in case he never saw her this close-up again. Then he kissed her once more—a kiss that was hot and urgent and hungry and exactly like the kissing of moments earlier when they could so easily have gone on and on.

Only this kiss was brief—he quickly ended it. Then

he got them both to their feet, took her hand and led her to the door.

Once it was open, he let go of her and leaned his spine to the door frame, watching from beneath hooded lids.

Hadley met his gaze, looking at the face that had embedded itself into her brain, into her thoughts, into her dreams more firmly now than even all those years ago when she'd had a crush on him. At the face of the man she never thought would want her, the man who wanted her so much at that moment that it showed in every line.

And she knew that if she stayed a minute longer she wasn't going to be able to go at all.

So she stepped out into the chilly night air and forced herself to walk across his deck and down the steps that led her away from him.

Carrying with her the feel of his lips on hers.

The memory of the warmth of his mouth on her breast.

And the intense need, deep inside, to finish what they'd started tonight.

In spite of everything else....

Chapter Nine

While Cody napped on Friday afternoon, Chase made business calls and Hadley went downstairs to the workroom.

Logan was set to return from his honeymoon on Saturday and Monday would be the first day that Logan, Chase and Hadley would actually get down to the business of furniture. Hadley wanted to go in armed with ideas for the unfinished pieces that had come in on the truck Chase had driven from New York, the pieces she already knew she would be upholstering in one way or another.

There were reviews of Mackey and McKendrick Furniture Designs that referred to what Chase and Logan produced as functional art. As Hadley looked things over, she understood the comment. What her brother and his best friend created was the kind of timeless, sturdy, practical, efficient furniture that would last generations. But these pieces were museum-quality art objects, as well.

She knew that there were some pieces that Chase and Logan collaborated on, and others that they came up with separately. She could tell the difference.

Logan's designs were more traditional, with a country appeal, a cottage charm.

Chase's designs were bolder, with a more modern edge to them.

The plan was for Hadley to contribute to the designs for the wooden-frame sofas and easy chairs that needed upholstery. For the pieces in which the hand-sanded wood not only provided the structure but also the aesthetic appeal in the arms, legs and sometimes the backs, she would be contributing seat cushions and pillows for comfort and to accentuate Logan's and Chase's vision.

Logan's pieces called for tapestries and plaids, for cozy prints, for warm, homey fabrics.

Chase's pieces shouted for leather—buttery-soft leather in dark, rich hues. Leather with so much give to it that to lie on a couch made of it would be like lying naked against a man's body, in a man's arms...

Oh, you really have to stop putting everything in those terms, she told herself.

But since leaving the loft the night before, thinking in

those terms was all she'd been able to do. About almost everything.

Sex on the brain—that's what she had and she couldn't seem to shake it.

Sex with Chase.

They'd come so close. And it had been so difficult for her to leave, to walk next door to her own apartment and go to bed alone, knowing he was within shouting distance. Knowing she could turn around, retrace her steps, knock on his door and just say let's do it...

But she hadn't. She wasn't quite sure how she'd managed not to, but she hadn't. And even after coaching Chase through Cody's breakfast and dressing the baby for the day, even after taking the baby for a walk together, playing with him together, feeding him lunch and deciding to take him to the high-school homecoming game tonight, here she was, still with sex on the brain.

What she should have been thinking about was how Chase had no intention of ever settling down with just one woman for longer than it took for the bloom to wear off of the relationship.

And that wasn't for her. Her relationship might have ended in divorce but that didn't mean that she'd given up on marriage. It was still what she wanted, what she hoped to do right the next time. And doing it right meant avoiding a man who thought of women as pearls he just kept adding to an endless string.

So what didn't happen last night shouldn't ever happen, she told herself. And not only because Chase wasn't marriage-minded. There were still the work, proximity and Logan issues, too.

But as she ran a hand over the curve of one of the chairs that was obviously Chase's design, as she felt the smoothness of the wood he'd carefully, lovingly shaped and sanded, she couldn't help thinking about his back, about how much she wanted to run her hands over it this same way...

She almost wished that the old crush was still in play, with all of its naïveté, with its blinders.

But it wasn't. It was long gone now. Replaced by a clear image of Chase as a flesh-and-blood man.

No illusions—he'd made sure that she had no illusions. Certainly none that her old crush would have afforded her.

But a reality check was good, she told herself.

And it was also good that things hadn't gone all the way last night. Good that her brother would be back tomorrow so she could get some distance from Chase, from Cody. So she could just do what she'd come home to Northbridge for and get on with her own life.

"It just can't be," she said out loud to that chair she was still fondling. "The man isn't even making any commitments to Cody."

Which was true—she could tell that Chase wasn't letting himself get too sucked into caring for the baby, and she thought that was because he was still allowing for the possibility of turning Cody over to one of his siblings if and when he located them.

He just wasn't a guy to bank on.

Sure, Chase was a great guy—every minute she spent with him taught her more about just how great a guy he was. Funny and charming, charismatic and kind, compassionate and intelligent and understanding.

That made for a great guy to be friends with. To work with. To hang around with. But that course shouldn't be varied from now.

Logan will be home tomorrow, she reminded herself again.

She just had to hold out until her brother got there.

Logan would be there to be Chase's friend and confidante, to be a glaring reminder of why a relationship between her and Chase was wrong. To provide a buffer zone between them.

A buffer zone.

That was a good thing, wasn't it?

That would keep her hands off Chase and his hands off her.

And yet in her mind she kept going back to the fact that Logan would be taking over with Cody.

That there wouldn't be any need for her to see Chase the way she had been.

To talk to him the way she had been.

To share any of the kind of closeness they had been—physical and otherwise.

And she couldn't believe how awful that prospect made her feel….

* * *

"Hogly? Woo! I heard you'd slimmed down but this is somethin' else!" a man shouted, as he and his date made their way toward Hadley in the bleachers.

"Oh, man, you did not just call her that…" Chase responded. "I can't believe how out of line you are. Apologize to her now—and then you need to work on getting your head out of—"

"Excuse him, he's had one too many," the woman said.

Hadley was tucking blankets around Cody in preparation for the walk back to the SUV after the Homecoming game Friday night. She straightened up to see the woman swat her partner's arm and say, "Go warm up the car. I'll be right there to drive you home."

"Not before he's apologized," Chase insisted, meeting the drunken man eye to eye.

"I'm sorry," the drunk said. "I thought I was paying her a compliment."

"Go! Before you make it worse," the woman shouted.

The couple looked vaguely familiar to Hadley but no names were coming to mind. And the fact that the man had referred to her as Hogly was no help—there had been a lot of venomous boys growing up who had adopted that version of her name to ridicule her for her weight. She'd done her best to ignore them, to focus on the fact that, for the most part, the people of Northbridge had not been hurtful. At least not intentionally.

Still, she wasn't sorry to see the lout go.

"I *am* sorry," the woman said more sincerely. "He can be a jerk sometimes, but what are you gonna do when you're married to them? It's these boring high-school games. He usually plays with the Bruisers and then he doesn't drink until after the game. But since the Bruisers sat this week out so the high school could have center stage for their Homecoming, here I am…"

The Bruisers were an informal sports team made up of the men in Northbridge. They got together to play basketball in the winter, baseball in the summer and football in the fall. The games had become a weekly tradition that most of the town turned out for, so Hadley had been to several since arriving in Northbridge. But she didn't recall seeing the man play.

Chase seemed at as much of a loss as she was, and it must have been clear from their expressions because then the woman said, "Amber. Amber Tamlyn—now Amber Berchord. And of course that would make my not-so-better-half Larry."

"Oh, right," Hadley said as she placed them both—cheerleader, quarterback, neither of them ever among the people who were very nice to her….

"We were gone all summer, taking care of Larry's father in Wyoming. We just got home and we've been hearing about how the furniture kings have moved back, and about you, Hadley, and how good you look now," Amber said.

Hadley wasn't sure what to say to that but she did

smile. A smile so tight it pinched, but a smile nonetheless. She'd considered what it would be like moving back to Northbridge before she'd done it, that not only would she encounter the people she liked, but also those she hadn't, those who had been unkind to her. In the end she'd decided that—as with any place she'd lived—she had to take the bad with the good.

And if she was going to live in the small town again, among even a few people who had been mean to her, she'd decided she was going to put her best face forward, that she wasn't going to hold a grudge. And that was what she was reminding herself when Amber Tamlyn turned to Chase.

"And you, Chase Mackey—where's your paunch and receding hairline?" Amber asked with a laugh, apparently referring to the changes that had overtaken her own husband.

"Yeah, I don't know, I guess they haven't caught up with me yet..." Chase said as if he wasn't any more sure than Hadley was how to respond to this woman.

Then Amber refocused on Hadley and said, "I heard you got married—is this little one yours?"

Hadley suddenly recalled that Amber Tamlyn had been the local gossip girl, that there wasn't much of anything she hadn't poked her nose into. And then reported on to everyone who would listen.

"Cody is my nephew," Chase contributed before Hadley could.

"But you did get married," Amber said to Hadley, as

if it had been a morsel of news that Amber had found hard to believe.

"I did," Hadley finally answered. "But I also got divorced."

"You couldn't have married anyone from around here or I would have heard…" Amber fished obviously for information.

"No, it was someone I met in college," Hadley answered, giving no more than she had to.

"And is that when you lost all the weight—after he left you?"

Okay, maybe some people deserved to have a grudge held against them…

"Who said he left her?" Chase retorted in the same tone he'd used to challenge Larry Berchord's name-calling.

More calmly, Hadley said, "As a matter of fact, I lost the weight right after leaving Northbridge." Then, deciding she'd had enough, Hadley added, "But as much as I'd love to talk, we really have to get Cody home."

"We? Are the two of you together?"

"Nice seeing you, Amber," Chase said facetiously rather than answer, cutting off any more of the encounter by picking up the stroller—baby and all—to carry it down the four steps to the ground.

"We did come together so he's my ride," Hadley informed the other woman to explain why she followed close on Chase's heels to make their abrupt escape.

They were barely out of the other woman's earshot

when Chase muttered, "Are you sure it was the right decision to come back to Northbridge?"

"There always have to be a few bad apples in the barrel," Hadley said. "But I've been here since June—I'm getting used to the shock over my weight and the fact that some of the things that get said are insensitive even when they aren't meant to be. I figure that eventually people will forget about the way things were and it'll pass. Besides, almost everyone in Northbridge is nice and friendly and has treated me really well. And you're getting welcomed with open arms."

"Just not by people I necessarily want to be welcomed by," he muttered.

It wasn't until they'd strapped the car seat into the SUV and Chase had them in line to get out of the school parking lot that he glanced at Hadley with a worried frown and said, "Are you okay?"

"Because of the Hogly thing? I'll admit that that's as bad as Homer Pritick calling you the mutt—it's not a name I'll ever like, but I'm okay. His wife is right— Larry Berchord was always a jerk, drunk or sober. Too bad for them both that he hasn't changed."

"Except for the potbelly and the hair loss," Chase reminded her with some satisfaction.

As they inched toward the exit, Chase glanced at her more intently and said, "Has it been weird for you? A change like that in the way you look?"

Hadley laughed. "Are you kidding? The weirdest! I'm used to it by now. But yes, being back in Northbridge, where it's a big deal all over again, reminds me of what it was like when I first lost the weight. When I first realized how different I look and that I was basically inhabiting a new body."

"What was it like…before? Was it like tonight all the time—that Hogly garbage?"

"Not all the time. Most people try to be sensitive. But the stares were almost as bad as the trash talk. And I hated that some people seemed to think the weight was an open invitation to tell me diet secrets or how much better I would look and feel if I slimmed down. Or that I shouldn't be eating something I was eating."

"And then, when the weight was gone?"

"Then it took a long time before it occurred to me that people—especially men—weren't looking at me because I was heavy, that they might be looking at me because I wasn't…"

"With lust in their hearts?" Chase joked.

"Yes," Hadley confirmed. "At first that seemed nice. And flattering. And it went to my head a little. Then I got sort of hostile—"

"Hostile?" he repeated, confused.

"I started to think that the same guys who were hitting on me after the weight loss hadn't wanted me before the weight loss—"

"And you were still the same person, so then it seemed like a looks-only thing. Like it wasn't you they wanted."

She didn't feel that way with Chase, whose attitude

toward her had always been kind and caring and positive. Plus, he never would have considered her someone
to date all those years ago because back then she was
too young for him to be interested in no matter what
she weighed.

"A looks-only thing, yes," she agreed.

They finally made it out of the parking lot and as they
set off for home, Chase took his eyes from the road to
look at her for a moment. Hadley had the sense that he
was carefully considering his next words.

Eventually, he said, "So, since Amber brought it up
and Logan never told me much, I don't know anything
about the guy you ended up marrying or about the whole
divorce thing."

"And now you want to?" she asked.

"Does it make me as bad as Amber if I say yes?"

"Only if you want to hear it so you can spread it
around."

"My lips are sealed," he swore.

And they were such nice lips, Hadley thought, trying
not to recall so vividly what they'd felt like on her breast
the previous night.

Or to want them there again…

"For instance," Chase was saying, "I have to assume
he wasn't one of the looks-only guys…"

"No, Garth didn't transfer in until my third year. By
then I'd lost all the weight and was just starting to have
a little confidence. And there he was—the new guy

everyone was talking about because he had this sort of edgy handsomeness and lots of style and panache..."

"I don't want to hear good things about him," Chase joked.

Hadley laughed. "There were a few—if there hadn't been I wouldn't have been with him. Although to be honest, all the other guys I knew had known me through the weight loss—which means I'd been heavy when I met them. The first time Garth laid eyes on me I looked the way I do now and it was...I don't know, kind of a kick to finally not be what I was tonight—the phenomenon of the fat girl who had lost a bunch of weight."

"It was a kick to just be the hot chick."

Hadley laughed. She was embarrassed to admit it, but she did. "Sort of."

Chase glanced at her again, appreciation in his eyes. "There's no sort of—you are definitely a hot chick."

"But I'm afraid that some of what drew me to Garth was that ego rush that came from the new shining star wanting me. It was the first time that had ever happened. I think it might have made me overlook some of his flaws."

"Such as?"

"His huge ego. And the need to have it constantly stroked—which I was good for because inside I was more grateful than—"

"Oh, I don't want to hear that, either," Chase said sadly. "Grateful? You felt grateful to be with him?"

Hadley shrugged. "It does some damage to grow up being called Hogly…"

"Oh, Had…" Chase muttered sympathetically.

"Anyway, I think I might have been a little too eager to please Garth. I ended up loving Italy and France and living there was an experience I wouldn't trade for anything now that I've done it, but no, it wasn't what I wanted to do. I did it because it was Garth's plan and as long as Garth wanted me, I would do anything he asked—including pack up and tag along all the way to Europe."

"But you were married to him by then, weren't you?"

"I was, we'd had a quickie wedding at the courthouse. But I'm not so sure that, for Garth, marrying me was anything more than a way to get his seamstress to Milan with him. I was dragging my feet about the move and his proposal was what put it over the top."

Chase glanced at her again, frowning. "You think he married you because you could sew?"

"It's not so far-fetched. Besides dating through design school, Garth and I figured out that we complemented each other when it came to work—where he was weak, I was strong, where I was weak, he was strong. We were both interested in fashion, but my designs could never compete with his—almost no one's could. But when it came to translating those designs to the real thing, he fell short. I had a knack for picking the perfect fabric, for turning his designs into the clothes he envisioned in a way that no one else did. We were a good team."

"And since I'm figuring his plan was to take Europe by storm, he needed the one person who could make his drawings come to life," Chase summarized.

"The one person at the time," Hadley amended. "So we went to Milan and we were both hired on by a couture house there. Later a house in Paris came knocking for him, and since I was still part of the package then, we both went there."

"But what about the marriage?"

"That was less of a success story. In Garth's eyes, marriage made me exclusive to him—professionally and personally. But he still saw himself as a free agent—"

"Professionally and personally?"

"Yeah," Hadley said quietly. "Early on, when he believed he needed me to sew for him, he was faithful. But once Paris came knocking and there were a couple of other seamstresses there who he thought could do him justice, too, he started to take my part for granted. He saw the need for my talents—and me—as less and less important. And with so many beautiful women all around him—"

"He decided to start sampling them," Chase guessed when her voice cracked with the memories of just how much her husband's infidelities had hurt.

"I was suspicious," Hadley continued after clearing her throat. "But whenever I confronted him he denied it. And—I'm not proud of this—I had a lot riding on being his wife, a lot of reasons to turn a blind eye to more than I should have—"

"Your whole career was connected to his, plus you were a long, long way from home."

"Right. So I let myself be convinced a few times that he was telling me the truth, that nothing was going on, that he really was working late in his studio, that he hadn't been with anyone else. But the last straw was when I caught him in bed with one of the models. That was it for me. That was when I filed for divorce."

A heavy silence fell for a few moments. But then she cast Chase a small smile and paraphrased what he'd said the night before. "And that's how I ended up exactly where you are—except that I had to go through a divorce and a lot of pain and misery to get there."

"I'm not the kind of guy who says I told you so," he said with an answering smile.

"But you would like to say that if I'd done it your way—without marriage—I could have just packed my bags, bought a plane ticket home and that would have been that."

His smile got slightly bigger but what he said was, "I hope that guy's career tanks without you."

Hadley laughed. "His last collection didn't do well and the reviews said that every piece was missing something, but no one could put their finger on what."

"You! It was missing you! That serves him right!"

There was definitely some satisfaction in thinking that, but Hadley refrained from saying it.

Besides, they'd arrived home by then and as Chase pulled into the garage Hadley switched mental gears. In thinking about tonight and trying to keep it from ending the way other evenings had ended with him, she'd formed a plan. A plan she'd begun to put into motion even before they'd left for the football game.

"So, Cody had his bath earlier," she said as Chase turned off the engine. "And he's already asleep. If you're careful, you can take off his coat and hat and change his diaper without waking him. Then just put him down for the night."

"Without you?"

"There's not really anything for me to do, and I think you're ready for a solo flight. It'll be easy."

Chase shook his head. "Sorry, but that's not going to work," he said, clearly not taking her seriously. "You were still downstairs but when the big guy got up from his nap this afternoon, he and I had a long talk—"

"Involving more than the word *oose?* Because that is the only word the big guy can say," Hadley reminded, playing along just to see where Chase was going with this.

Chase shook his head again. "That oose thing? That's just a con job. When the big guy has something to say, look out! You can't shut him up."

"And what did he have to say this afternoon?"

"That he wanted me to do something special to thank you for everything you've done for us. He was all over me about how I'd dropped the ball when it came to that.

He really let me have it. But he had a whole plan for what I'm supposed to do tonight after we put him to bed and if you don't let me go through with it there's no telling what I'll be in for from him tomorrow. The kid has no mercy."

"And you're crazy," Hadley said with a laugh.

"It isn't me," he insisted, sticking to his charade. "It's all Cody. He went on and on about how you've been there for us day and night, how you've done most of the work, how—if it wasn't for you—I would have probably fed him beer and peanuts, and he wouldn't have survived. He even has a gift for you…"

"The diaper is dirty, isn't it? You smelled it when you put him in the car seat and you're just trying to lure me up to your place to get me to change it."

"Do the sniff test yourself. This is the honest-to-God truth," he said, grinning but not wavering in his game. "It's all the Code-man's deal, I'm just doing his bidding. He's the boss here."

Then Chase's grin turned softer, and he said, "Besides, this is the last night we'll be on our own. You're not really gonna keep us from having it, are you?"

"That depends on what we're having," Hadley said wryly.

"We're having wine and our last few hours before things change," he said with just a hint of melancholy. "And that's it. I give you my word. As your brother's best friend."

That sounded like a vow he intended to keep. And yet

she still knew the safest course was to say no. It was the only sure way to make it through this time she'd spent with him without adding another complication to what they'd both already agreed was complicated enough.

But the safest course just wasn't the one she could make herself take tonight...

"Cody bought wine?" she heard herself say.

"And a thank-you present. I'm telling you, the kid has layers you wouldn't believe."

"And you'll behave?" she challenged.

Chase smiled. "I've thought it through, and even though I've had one hell of a time remembering it, you're my best friend's sister. And that's a line that shouldn't be crossed. At least not any more than I already have."

She thought he meant that.

And it disappointed her more than seemed possible.

But maybe they really would be able to come through this just as good friends...

"So this is all Cody's idea, huh?" she said.

"Scout's honor."

Hadley hesitated.

But one way or another Chase was right—they did only have tonight before everything changed.

And she couldn't pass it up.

Chapter Ten

Hadley was surprised by what she found when she and Chase arrived at his loft after the Homecoming game.

Just as they were leaving earlier in the evening he'd said he'd forgotten his keys. He'd asked her to take Cody downstairs to put the baby in the car seat while he went back inside to get them.

It seemed to have taken him longer than it should have. And when they got back to the loft, she realized what he'd been up to—he'd used that time to prepare logs in the fireplace to be lit, to set out wine, glasses and a small gift box on the coffee table.

"What's all this?" she whispered so she wouldn't wake Cody, nodding in the direction of the set stage.

Chase smiled a small smile. "Cody must have sent

elves over while we were gone—I told you, the kid had a plan for tonight. And I'm doing whatever it takes to put him to bed so just make yourself comfortable."

They'd brought the eleven-month-old inside in the car seat. Chase set the baby down long enough to take off the leather baseball jacket he was wearing.

Hadley also removed her coat, but rather than staying behind, she followed Chase as he took Cody into the nursery.

She didn't go all the way into the room, though. She stopped at the doorway and merely watched from there as Chase carefully handled the sleeping infant, laying him gently in the crib where he took off the baby's cold-weather gear.

From her position, Hadley could see man and baby. Cody seemed so tiny under the ministering of Chase's big hands. Taking Cody's small arms from his jacket sleeves, Chase rolled the infant from one side to the other. He finally got the coat out from under him before going on to change his diaper.

Chase was no longer daunted by handling Cody and Hadley realized she could turn over Cody's care to him without concern.

She also realized that she wasn't altogether eager to do that. And that there was some sadness to not being needed by them.

But she reminded herself that she'd done what she was supposed to do—she'd taught Chase how to take care of his nephew—and tried to chase away her own glumness.

"Sleep tight, big guy," Chase whispered to Cody after he'd tucked the baby in.

Then he turned to Hadley and motioned with a jut of his dimpled chin for her to go into the living room.

Hadley took a deep breath as she did, wavering in her resolve after only those few minutes of watching him. The mere sight of the man just got to her and there didn't seem to be anything she could do about it. Except stay away. And she was already not doing that…

In the living room, Chase started the fire that Hadley knew wasn't going to help her already-elevated temperature. Then he opened and poured the wine.

She accepted her glass and sat as far from the flames as she could, taking one end of the leather couch.

Chase handed her the small, beribboned box from the coffee table and then took his own wine with him to sit as far from her as he could get at the opposite end of the sofa.

She hadn't expected that.

And wished she wasn't so let down by it.

"So this is from Cody?" she asked.

"Yep," Chase confirmed. "It's to say thanks for all you've done. Open it."

Hadley untied the ribbon and lifted the lid. Inside was a delicate bracelet made of two thin pieces of wood— one light, the other darker—coiled intricately around each other.

"I don't think Cody did this," she said with a hint of awe as she took the bracelet out of the box to look more closely at the simple, elegant piece before she slipped it around her wrist. "How did you do this with wood?"

Chase shrugged. "Some moist heat makes it pliable— I can do just about anything with it that way."

"It's beautiful," Hadley said quietly, studying it, touched by the work that had to have gone into it and even more impressed by his talent. By him.

"Cody'll be glad you liked it," Chase said, deflecting her compliment.

"When did you have time to make this?"

"Oh, you know, there was a need for some winding down last night and for some thinking through some things and…well, I think better when I work, and that's what came out of it."

"You were up all night thinking, huh?" she said. "What about?"

"You know what I was thinking about," he challenged with a slightly huskier note to his voice.

"And were your thoughts going round and round like the two pieces of wood?"

"Pretty much," he said with a wry chuckle.

"And your thoughts ended up at me being Logan's sister," she said, noting how far he sat from her on the couch.

"Pretty much," he repeated, this time without the chuckle.

"What if I wasn't?" she asked, making it sound as

if she were merely curious, when the truth was, at that moment, she was wishing things were different. "What if I was just any girl?"

Chase laughed. "You're a long way from just any girl no matter what. But don't ask me what I'd do if you were—that's tempting fate at this point," he said.

"I did ask you, though."

"I wouldn't be sitting over here, that's for sure. But you are Logan's sister. You'll always be Logan's sister…"

Hadley understood what he was saying. But that still didn't keep her from thinking that there he was—so handsome she couldn't get her eyes off of him, so sexy she could hardly stand it.

And so far, far away when she just wanted him so much nearer…

"You know," she heard herself say before she'd thought it through, as if something stronger than she was pushing her. "One of the things that has to happen for us all to be here together is that we have to live our own lives, and we absolutely have to mind our own business. I don't expect Logan to tell me everything and I don't intend to tell him everything. Do you?"

"Logan and I have never had any secrets," Chase said as if that was one of the things he'd considered during his sleepless night. "And living here like we all are isn't going to allow for much privacy. We're gonna have a pretty good idea what's going on with each other."

"But what if there's just tonight and after tonight you and I…aren't…"

He laughed as if she had to be joking, even as Hadley wondered herself at what she was saying. At why she couldn't let this lie when he was making it so easy for her to. Was it that he seemed unavailable again?

But that would mean that this had something to do with the old crush and she knew that wasn't really the case. Yes, this was the guy she'd fantasized about for years growing up. But since those fantasies had been relatively innocent and had never gone beyond kissing, they'd already been satisfied and basically put to rest.

What was calling her at that moment was all about what had sprung to life between them since Chase had come back to Northbridge. This was about the way he made her feel now. About how much she wanted the man she now knew him to be.

It was the present-day Chase who made her laugh. The present-day Chase who had helped reboot the self-confidence that had floundered after she found her husband in bed with someone else. The present-day Chase she wanted.

And if the present-day Chase was opposed to marriage and commitment?

That didn't matter since it wasn't marriage or commitment she was thinking about tonight.

"A one-night stand?" Chase was saying, echoing her own thoughts. "That can't be what you're talking about. Your brother would shoot me."

"It isn't about my brother. And he wouldn't shoot you if he never knew..."

Had she said that out loud?

She had.

And then she was also saying, "I'm an adult and what I choose to do isn't for Logan to have any say in."

"Oh, Had..." Chase said, laughing, shaking his head, tempted—she could see that—but also leery and hesitant. "You can't be serious."

"I can. If I want to."

"Are you just trying to prove something?" he asked, sounding slightly crestfallen at that prospect.

"No, I'm not just trying to prove something," she said sincerely. "But you're right—these are the last few hours we have before things change. The last few hours when Logan isn't here. I haven't been able to stop thinking about that all day. And Logan definitely shouldn't be a factor when he isn't even here."

Chase studied her and she could tell there was a lot going through his mind, too. Then he smiled slightly while still frowning a little, and said, "Are you trying to seduce me, Ms. McKendrick?"

"I know I'm not very good at it..."

Somewhere along the way she'd put her wineglass on the coffee table and brought her legs onto the couch, curled to one side so she was facing Chase. He had only to bend forward to grasp her legs and pull them out from under her so he could also pull her toward him.

Closer, looking steadfastly into her face, he said in a quiet voice, "No games—just talk to me, Had."

"That's exactly it—it isn't more talking that I want," she said back, equally quietly. "We only have this one last night. Then Logan will be home and everything will be about more than you and me. But tonight there's still just you and me. Nothing bigger than that—not relationships or commitments or anything. You and me with a built-in time limit. I kind of don't want to waste that."

"And when tomorrow comes?"

"Then everything will just go on."

"And no one will be the wiser? We'll act like it never happened?" he asked dubiously.

"It'll just be between the two of us," Hadley said decisively. "But at least we will have had this…"

He frowned and she prepared herself, certain that he was going to say no. That his friendship with her brother meant more to him than one night with her.

Then he raised a hand to the back of her head and gently pulled her closer.

"I've never wanted anything so damn bad in my life," he confided in a way that made her think that he'd been maintaining quite a facade since they'd reached the loft. A facade that had suddenly been removed. "But you have to be sure you are okay with it."

She was acutely aware that he was risking more than she was. And the fact that he was still willing to do it in order to have her was heady.

"One night. Just tonight. I'm sure," she told him,

knowing that if she didn't have this one night with him she would be left wondering what it would have been like, longing for it, imagining it, fantasizing about it, maybe forming an all-new crush on him that could only be detrimental to everything from here on.

He slid both of his hands into the back of her hair and brought her head up so he could look into her eyes.

And that was when she knew that he wasn't capable of saying no to her. That he wanted her with the same kind of raw hunger that she wanted him, the kind of raw hunger that demanded it have its day.

Then he kissed her, lips parted, tongue coming out almost instantly. He kissed her with a sudden intensity that made her marvel at how he'd ever waited. Or maybe because he had, that kiss was all the more red-hot right from the start. But red-hot it was, and Hadley answered it with a heat of her own.

And then he ended it, took her hand and led her to his bedroom, where autumn moonlight cast a milky glow through a skylight.

They stood beside his enormous bed with its downy quilt making it look like a big cloud and took their shoes and socks off. Then Chase focused solely on Hadley, replacing his hands in her hair to hold her to another kiss that mimicked the first.

Hadley raised her hands to his chest but almost immediately resented the flannel of his shirt barricading her from him, so she wasted no time in unbuttoning it, in shedding it, in placing her hands on the bare skin of brawny pectorals.

But Chase seemed in no hurry himself now as he went on kissing her more thoroughly than she'd ever been kissed, cradling her head in his hands.

Hadley consciously slowed down, too, savoring his kiss, savoring the feel of his naked chest. If they were only going to have tonight, she wanted to make it last, too.

About the time she thought that, Chase took his hands from her hair and moved to the buttons of her sweater, unfastening them and pulling it off her arms.

Then, as if he had to do it, he looked down at the camisole that remained—a lacy veil that left little to the imagination since she'd worn no bra tonight.

A grin lit up Chase's handsome face and he apparently liked the hint of lace over her nakedness so well that rather than remove it, he went back to kissing her and began work on jeans instead—maneuvering hers off but only unbuttoning and unzipping his own.

That made Hadley smile into the playfully sexy kiss they were sharing before she took over and removed his pants and boxers, too.

When that was accomplished he swept her up into his arms and laid her on the quilt.

And Hadley got her first chance to look at him, just as he drank in the sight of her in the mere scraps of lace she still wore—the tank top and thong.

Yes, she'd seen him at the swimming pool years ago.

But that was nothing compared to what he'd become as a man. Broad, strong shoulders. Well-cut biceps. Flat, defined stomach. Narrow hips. Long, thick legs. And evidence of just how much he wanted her....

Too much to stay away.

He joined her on the bed, beside her, a thigh across hers as he kissed her again, a profoundly intimate, no-holds-barred kiss full of promise as one hand found her breast, answering a need that had been gaining ground in Hadley.

But at that moment she silently cursed the lace for providing the same kind of obstacle his flannel shirt had.

Chase must have had a similar thought because just then he slipped his hand underneath the fabric, clasping her breast in the warm embrace of that big hand.

A sigh escaped Hadley's throat at that skin-to-skin contact, at once again being within his expert grasp. Almost as if he had a sixth sense, he knew exactly when to apply pressure, when to knead, when to tease, when to concentrate his attention on the taut kernel of her nipple, circling it, flicking at it, even giving it the most tender of tugs and pinches.

Writing—she was actually writhing beneath his touch as their kissing became all the more intense, all the more forceful and passionate.

Driven by a need to imprint every moment, every sensation, onto her memory, Hadley explored his body with her hands, reveling in the textures of his skin, the solidness of the muscles beneath it, the shape and size and slope and magnificence of it all.

Then he deserted her mouth and moved lower, finding her breast, rekindling the sensations of the night before and adding to them with an all-new abandon, using that wicked, wicked tongue to tantalize her, torment her and turn her on even more.

Her back arched and he used that moment to finally take off the camisole, his mouth abandoning her breast for only a split second.

And when he came back again his hand went on a leisurely journey down her stomach to hook fingers into the lace of her panties.

Off they came, too, leaving her completely exposed and somehow not the least self-conscious when he paused a second time to look at her.

His only compliment was a groan, but there was such appreciation in it that it just made her smile as he pressed his lips to her navel and then kissed his way to her other breast to take it into the warm, wet silk of his mouth.

His hand was on her side and it coursed a path downward, to her hip, to her thigh, to that spot between her legs that was growing rapidly more needy.

Tender strokes and discoveries of oh-so-sensitive spots were only the beginning as fingers gave previews of things to come.

Hadley reached for him, too, enclosing that long, hard staff in a grip she offered softly at first, then with more tenacity, eager to learn that part of him, too.

The groan that answered her touch came from deep in his throat and suddenly his mouth was gone from her breast, leaving a chill chased away when he dropped kisses like pearls down her belly.

All the way down until his mouth replaced his hand there, too, surprising her a little before he showed her delights that caused an all-new, near-frantic need to erupt in her.

A need so great it made her moan this time.

And then he was up and gone, stretching across her to the nightstand for protection.

A mere moment seemed like hours but then he was there again, lying on his side, bringing her to lie on hers to face him.

His hand was on her thigh, pulling her leg over his hip and bringing her close. Close enough for him to find his home inside of her, carefully easing into her, fitting them together flawlessly.

He kissed her again, pulsing within her, as he began to move. Slowly, rhythmically at first, Hadley met him, tightening around him. Then with some speed but still in harmony, meeting and parting in an intimate choreography of bodies that grew increasingly receptive to every movement, more and more in tune with each other.

And the more in tune with each other they were, the faster the pace—rapid and forceful and wild.

So wild that it took Hadley somewhere she hadn't been before, raising her higher and higher until she broke through to something she'd never completely reached in the past, until what erupted all through her sent her into a mindless bliss that stole her breath and her ability to move, to do anything more than hold on to Chase as he made it go on and on and on in incredible, glorious rapture.

Rapture that peaked and then found a second foothold to peak again when he grasped her derriere to pull her nearer still, to plunge so deeply inside of her for his own climax that they were melded together while wave after wave washed over them both.

One final shudder, one final tightening of Chase's arms around her, of hers around him, and everything wound down like a clock coming to a halt.

Chase rested his chin atop her head and breathed a breath he must have been holding, too, and Hadley could feel his heart racing against hers.

For a time that was how they stayed—arms and legs entwined, clasped together seamlessly. Then Chase kissed her head, flexed a little inside of her before he slipped out and rolled to his back, taking her with him so that her head could rest on his chest.

"I need the whole night," he whispered in a gravelly voice.

It hadn't occurred to her to leave so she just laughed and said, "Okay."

"And a catnap," he added.

She laughed again and craned her head back so she could look up at him. "Wore you out, did I?"

He grinned. "Just a catnap," he insisted as if she had challenged him. "And then we'll see…"

He kissed her head once more before letting his drop back as if it were too heavy to keep up, but his hand went on running from her elbow to her shoulder, her shoulder to her elbow, in a whisper of a massage.

Fatigue began to weigh her down, too, and Hadley closed her eyes, suddenly feeling as if this all might not be real.

But it was real, she told herself as she settled so perfectly against the warmth of his body.

She and Chase Mackey had just made love.

And if anything had far and away surpassed her old fantasies of him and left them in the dust, it was that.

Chapter Eleven

Three weeks.

"I think I'm gonna go out of my mind," Chase confided to Cody as he finished putting on the baby's pajamas and laid him in the crib.

It had been three weeks since Logan, Meg and Tia had returned from their honeymoon. Three weeks since the night that Chase had spent with Hadley. Three weeks that he, Hadley, Logan and Logan's small family had all lived closely together, worked together, eaten most meals together.

Three weeks during which Chase and Hadley had both kept the agreement they'd made after an entire night of lovemaking—to act publicly and privately as if nothing had happened between them, as if they were no more than acquaintances who worked together, who had Logan in common.

Three weeks since that entire night of lovemaking that had been the best damn night—and lovemaking—of Chase's life.

Three weeks that had been the worst three weeks he'd ever lived through.

Not that there had been anything outwardly wrong with them. It was good to again have Logan's day-to-day input and the closer teamwork that had begun their business, that had been in shorter supply while Logan was in Connecticut and Chase was in New York.

And having Hadley do their upholstering was also the right move—she was insightful, talented, productive. She brought fresh ideas and viewpoints into the mix, and she was good at what she did. Even if she had been very, very quiet.

Plus there was the family atmosphere of having Logan's new wife and his three-year-old daughter, Tia, around—that translated into extra hands with Cody, into Tia entertaining the infant and Meg babysitting during the workday, which all helped out. There had even been a family party for Cody's first birthday the week before.

So on the surface, things looked great.

But under the surface Chase was being eaten up inside by having to see Hadley, be with Hadley, work with Hadley, talk to Hadley—all on the most superficial terms and as if nothing else had ever gone on.

"I don't know what's wrong with me," he told Cody, leaning on the crib rail to look down at the sleepy infant who had one arm wrapped around his stuffed moose and the thumb of his other hand in his mouth as he stared up with big brown eyes at his uncle.

"It's just never been anything like this. This is…I don't know what this is. I'm tellin' you, little man, I've never been through anything like it. And now I know she's downstairs, workin' in the shop, and I'm up here, and I want her so bad I don't know how much longer I can stand it…"

Cody's eyelids were getting visibly heavy but the baby seemed to fight it as if he knew Chase needed to vent. He also removed his thumb from his mouth and offered it to Chase as consolation.

Even in his misery, that made Chase laugh. "Thanks," he said. "But that's okay, you can keep your thumb. This isn't your problem, it's mine."

Chase smoothed a hand over the infant's spiky hair, ridiculously touched by the kid's offer. Cody had gotten to him, too, he realized. He didn't understand any of it, but as far as Cody was concerned, there was at least an easy fix.

When he'd inherited Cody he'd felt as if the door was open for him to potentially pass the baby on to one of his younger siblings as soon as he found them. He was still having trouble reaching his sister, Shannon Duffy, and had yet to find out anything about his twin brothers, but the longer he had Cody, the more concrete became the idea of not passing him on to anyone.

No one could possibly be as surprised by that as Chase was, but it was true.

Yes, taking care of the baby was a lot of work. Yes, it tied Chase down. Yes, he knew he was signing on for a long-term relationship with someone. A long-term relationship that he knew would have its ups and downs.

But he really did care about this baby. He cared what happened to him. He felt driven to make sure that Cody had a decent, happy life, to provide that for him.

So while he hadn't yet told even Logan, he supposed he'd decided to do what his older sister had wanted—he was going to raise her son.

That was the easy fix with Cody.

But with Hadley?

Not such an easy fix…

Rubbing Cody's head was making it impossible for the baby to stay awake despite the fact that he was still trying to.

Chase leaned over the rail, kissed the infant's forehead and said, "Go ahead and go to sleep."

Then Chase stepped away from the crib and turned off the overhead light so the room had only the glow of a night-light to illuminate it.

When he glanced back at Cody, he found that the infant had already fallen into a peaceful slumber.

Lucky kid, Chase thought, knowing that tonight—like every night since the one he'd spent with Hadley—he would toss and turn and stare at the ceiling and think of her and wish she were there with him and ultimately get very little rest.

He switched on the baby monitor, took the receiver with him, left Cody's room and instantly thought again about Hadley being just downstairs.

Maybe some air would help.

Setting the baby monitor on the table near the door, he went out onto the deck, not bothering to put on a coat over his flannel shirt and ignoring the cold of the early October night. Instead he crossed the deck so he could peer over its railing at the window of the workshop below.

The light was still on.

Hadley was definitely still there.

And even though he couldn't see anything but the white glow of shop light coming through the window, he kept staring at it as if he could see her.

He'd never been so obsessed with anyone. He wanted her so damn bad he ached. And not only did he want her in bed, he wanted to walk out of Cody's room and have her waiting for him in the kitchen or on the couch like she had all those evenings when Logan was on his honeymoon. He wanted to talk to her. Laugh with her. He just wanted to have her to himself!

That was a huge problem with the way things were, he thought. He never got to be alone with Hadley. There was always Logan or Meg or Logan and Meg. There was Tia. And Cody. There was never just Hadley. And he was discovering that he craved that as much as he craved touching her again, holding her again, kissing her, taking her to bed…

He wanted every bit of it.

He wanted it right now.

And he wanted it from here on, without having to hide anything, without any time limit—built-in or otherwise—without any end at all…

Is that true? he asked himself when it struck him that he'd actually had that thought. Did he want Hadley from here on, without end? Because that went against everything he'd ever considered when he'd thought about women or his own future.

Having Hadley from here on, without end was…

"Marriage," he said out loud, scornfully.

But when he thought about marriage in terms of Hadley, he somehow didn't feel the kind of scorn he'd always felt about the subject before.

And that was hard to believe.

"Jeez, are you forgetting the Pritcks?" he asked himself as if he were talking to someone else.

But he wasn't forgetting them. Or any of the other numerous examples of marriage-gone-bad that had fueled his opinion of the institution.

It was just that he didn't see himself and Hadley in any of those examples.

"This is why people do it," he said when it dawned on him.

People got married because they felt the way he felt

at that moment—he wanted Hadley, he didn't want anything or anyone to ever keep her away from him or take
her away from him, and it didn't seem possible for what
they had to ever go bad.

But it would change, he reasoned. He knew it would.
Relationships always changed.

Only not always for the worst—that's what Hadley
had said.

Relationships did change, he knew that from his
friendship with Logan. It had changed when Logan
had married the first time. And not all the changes had
been good—Chase had hated that Logan had moved
to Connecticut to be with his Yale professor wife, that
he'd opened a workshop and showroom there. Even if
it had been good for business, it had still meant that he
and Logan hadn't seen as much of each other, that the
way they worked had been interrupted.

Some of the fun had gone out of their friendship
then. Logan hadn't been around for happy hour after
work whenever the mood had struck. Logan hadn't
been around for Sunday afternoon football anymore.
He hadn't been around for going clubbing or to the mov-
ies or to football or basketball or baseball games at the
drop of a hat.

But none of that had changed their friendship. Yes,
they'd made alterations to accommodate what had
changed, but the friendship itself hadn't changed. Because no matter what, there was still a bond between
them. What had made them friends long, long ago was

still the glue that held them together through anything that happened.

So why couldn't the same thing be true of a good marriage?

Chase suddenly discovered a part of him that wanted to believe—that was willing to believe—that that was possible.

But only when he thought of Hadley as his partner in it.

There had never been another woman with whom he'd been willing to weather change. Another woman whom he'd been interested in having around once the newness wore off.

But in most ways Hadley was already not new, and that hadn't altered in the slightest how hot he was for her. It was actually another thing he liked, something else that made their whole relationship feel good, feel right.

And another thing she'd said came to mind, too— something about relationships mellowing with age—and for the first time in his life even the thought of a relationship aging, mellowing like a great wine, becoming as comfortable and comforting as his favorite pair of jeans, appealed to him.

Hadley was just different. There was just something about her that made her special.

That last night they'd had together, when she'd been trying to seduce him, when she'd asked how things might be if she was just any girl—he'd told her that she was a long way from just any girl, and he'd meant that. Not only had he meant that she wasn't just any girl because she was Logan's sister—which was what she'd been asking. But even when Chase had said it he'd meant it as more than that. Hadley wasn't just any girl. Not to him.

Yes, she was beautiful and challenging and fun and smart and sweet and sassy and sexy. But Hadley also brought out things in him that no one else ever had, a side of him that he didn't expose to anyone—including Logan. She was the safest haven he'd ever found. She filled a gap he'd had his entire life. And just being with her made him stronger. It made him feel whole.

Which was why, when he thought about the long-term, when he thought about their relationship evolving, when he thought about change and even hardship, he also thought that having Hadley by his side would only help.

Hell, when he thought about it, it occurred to him that he actually liked the idea of the changes he was envisioning with her, of raising Cody with her, of having kids of their own to raise, of aging with her.

He liked the idea of working with Logan, of still having the friendship they'd always had. But at the end of a long workday, he wanted to go off alone with Hadley not as his friend's sister, but as his own wife. As the woman he shared his life with. He liked the idea of having a life with her that involved the two of them separate from anyone else. He liked the idea of having an entire future with her.

A future that needed to start right now, because he couldn't go another damn minute pretending that she was nothing more to him than his friend's sister, than his coworker.

He spun away from the deck railing, went back into the loft, closed the door and snatched up the receiver to the baby monitor. He knew it transmitted to the work-room, because when Meg had errands to run she put Cody down for his nap here and left the receiver with him so he could hear Cody stir.

And now with that in hand, he headed for the stairs that would take him down to the shop.

To Hadley.

And hopefully to the rest of his life with her...

"Had! We have to talk."

Startled, Hadley looked up from a piece of tapestry she was working on at her cutting table to find Chase at the foot of the steps that led down from his loft.

Wasn't it bad enough to have to see him as much as she did? The reason she was in the shop at eight o'clock at night was to work without finding her gaze constantly wandering to him, without the sight of his hands caus-ing her mind to drift off into memories of what it had felt like to have those hands on her naked skin, without being tortured by being near him and having to act as if every nuance, every sound of his voice, everything about him didn't affect her.

"Logan told you," she said when her fright had calmed, guessing at what had prompted this visit when neither of them had sought out the other alone since Logan, Meg and Tia had come home from Disneyland.

Chase's expression turned puzzled. "Logan told me what?"

"That I'm leaving."

"Leaving?"

If Logan hadn't told him what she'd just informed her brother of tonight after dinner, then why was Chase here?

She didn't have another guess, and rather than asking, she decided it was better to focus on her own plans. So she said, "I have some friends in New York who I'm going to stay with for a while. I might see about signing on with the design house they work for…"

She didn't offer an explanation. Surely it was obvious in her quiet, distracted, owlish, out-of-sorts mood of the past three weeks that she'd been wrong when she'd told him that she would be able to merely go on as if nothing had happened. So wrong…

The confused expression on Chase's handsome face made it clear that he was having some difficulty registering what she'd just told him but she went on anyway. "I'll stay until you can find someone else to do your upholstering. But I called the dry cleaners in town and they gave me a list of people around here who sew.

There are quite a few of them. I don't think you'll have too much of a problem—"

Chase held up a hand to stop her from going on. "I haven't talked to Logan tonight so, no, I didn't know you'd told him that. But…no!" Chase nearly shouted.

"No?" Hadley repeated.

Chase crossed the expanse of the workshop to stand on the other side of her cutting table. Hadley did what she tried so hard not to do all the rest of the time—she looked directly at him, drinking in the view of that masculine perfection that she'd always compared other men to. It was unbearable to see him, to feel the way she did—which was so much more powerful than that adolescent crush had ever felt—to want him with every ounce of her being, and yet not be able to run into his arms.

"I'm figuring that you want to leave because this isn't working any better for you than it is for me," Chase said.

"I can honestly say that taking the constant abuse and being the brunt of jokes as the heavy girl in middle school and high school was a picnic compared to the last three weeks," she replied. Compared to the torment of learning how terrific things with him really could be and then needing to deny herself ever having those things again.

"Well, I've been going out of my mind, Had," Chase said. "And I just can't do it anymore."

He went on to tell her that he'd just now had a revelation. About her, about wanting her, about wanting a relationship, a future—marriage—with her...

"I'm gonna keep Cody," he also told her. "Maybe it's the air in Northbridge or something, but all of a sudden I want the whole family thing. I'll go on trying to reach my sister, trying to find my brothers, but even when I find them I'll still keep Cody, give him a home and the kind of life I wanted as a kid. And I want you to be a part of that, too. I want us to be a family. I even want us to have kids of our own," he said as if he was surprised by his own conclusions.

Then he frowned at her. "Why are you shaking your head?"

Hadley hadn't even been aware that she was.

She stopped. But that didn't make her any more receptive to what he was suggesting.

"That isn't you, Chase," she said simply.

"What isn't me?"

"I can understand why you've decided to keep Cody, to give him the kind of life you wanted as a kid and didn't have—it's the only way you make absolutely sure that he gets it. I hope you can do it, that you can stick with it—"

"Although you don't really think I can," he interpreted her tone.

"I think it's possible, especially being here with Logan and Meg and Tia, where you'll have help, where things are already kid-friendly, where you and Logan can be raising kids together at the same time—"

"But even if I can make it as a parent…"

"Marriage is not for you—that's what you said," Hadley reminded him.

"And what I thought until tonight."

"Chase…" She was aware that she was shaking her head again but she didn't stop. "I know you just got back to Northbridge and maybe I look like the only game in town, but after a while you'll see that that isn't the case and you'll have to sample all the fruits that Northbridge has to offer. And then Billings and who knows where after that. Just the way you always have because you made the decision long ago that that's how you truly want to live your life."

"Now I've made another decision that cancels that one out," he insisted.

Hadley did more headshaking, feeling as if she were made of glass that had many, many cracks, that she could crumble at any time.

"You said yourself that you don't believe in marriage," she said quietly, remorsefully. "You've based your life on that. Devoted yourself to it. Fought for it in court! A belief that strong doesn't blow away in the wind."

"All I know is that tonight I decided that I can believe in marriage with you," he declared firmly.

"With me? As if I'm somehow different? As if I'm the one woman who could change your mind? Change what you've been convinced is the only way for you to be happy?"

"Don't say it like it's impossible," he countered, frowning darkly at her. "You're great! Great and, yes, different. You are the one woman who could change my mind, who makes me so damn happy that I want to hang on to it, to you. For the first time in my life, you have me thinking that marriage isn't a one-way ticket to misery and drudgery and regret."

"The one woman," she repeated, honestly unable to feel as if she of all people could have had that kind of impact on this man. "Even if you do believe that right now," she went on, "I don't believe that it will last. I think that after a while, when the bloom has worn off, you'll just be doing what you said you don't want to be doing—being annoyed by the little things rather than really wanting me. I think that given a little time—"

"What we have now will change and mellow with age—that's what you said," he reminded her of her words the way she'd reminded him of his. "Well, here's a news flash for you—I considered that the bloom would wear off and I was okay with that when it came to you. In fact, when I pictured it with you, I even liked the idea of settling in, of having you by my side for all the changes I could think of and for any I couldn't. I liked the idea of having you by my side raising Cody and our own kids and for everything that could possibly come our way—good or bad."

Hadley was beginning to have an idea of her own about where this had originated. "So this came to you when you decided to keep Cody."

"The decision to keep Cody has been brewing."

"And when you made it, you also made the decision that maybe marriage—to me—might be the right thing, too. It's okay, deciding to keep him is huge. It's no wonder—"

"This wasn't a share-the-load decision. I'm not Homer Pritick thinking to get himself a woman to cook and clean and do his laundry while he worked the fields. Even without Cody, I'd be standing here saying these same things to you because—"

"Because there are some big shake-ups in your life—moving back to the isolation of Northbridge, learning that nothing about the beginning of your life was the way you've always thought it was. Plus when you and Logan made the choice to come back here, you didn't bargain for Logan finding a wife the first week he was here, and now he has someone and you—"

"No! None of that has any more to do with this than Cody does!" he shouted. "It's you I'm going out of my mind without. It's you I want to get away from the rest of it to be with. It's just you I want!"

For now maybe that was true, Hadley thought. But only for now. Because as she stood there staring at him, she saw again what she'd seen when they were kids—Chase with one girl after another. She heard again the mentions Logan had made of Chase with one woman after another over the years. She recalled too vividly his own words when he'd told her how determined he was not to stay with anyone once the relationship became tedious.

In her memory she also saw her former husband the way she'd seen him the day she'd walked into her own bedroom and found him in bed with someone else.

And in her heart—alongside all the feelings she had for Chase, alongside what she wanted so badly it was eating her alive—she believed that with a man like him, she would end up once more left behind for the pursuit of other women.

And she could not—she would not—be that again. No matter how much it hurt to be denying herself the opportunity to have him.

So she looked him squarely in the eye, took a deep breath and in a voice that shook and cracked and gave away just how difficult this was for her, she said, "No, Chase, I'm sorry, but no. It just wouldn't work out—I know it wouldn't. Even committing to raising Cody isn't the same as making a commitment to me, to marriage. Cody will grow up and go out on his own, but a lifelong commitment to me—"

"Lifelong—yes, that's exactly what I want with you!" he swore.

She shook her head in denial again and went on with what she was going to say. "You're the first person to point out how unlikely that is—you have honestly believed for as long as you can remember that marriage makes people miserable. And think about what it means if things don't work out between us—right now I can walk away, I can go to New York while you stay here with Logan and your business. No one still has to know what's gone on and there's no harm done. But if you and I got married and then—"

She'd almost said what she was thinking: and then you cheated or wanted out because marriage really isn't for you...

She settled on, "—and then it didn't work out, Logan would be caught in the middle, your business would be caught in the middle and real damage would be done. Far-reaching damage. Neither of us can let that happen."

"Then we won't let that happen," he contended.

"Chase..."

"Your brother is like blood to me, Hadley. He's more to me that those real brothers or sisters I just found out I have. I don't take that lightly. Until now I would have said that there wasn't anything that I would put that at risk for. But given the choice between my friendship with Logan and you?" He shook his head firmly, giving no quarter on this subject. "I'm standing here right now, in front of you, telling you that I choose you. And that's something you can't take lightly. I can make that commitment to you with so much at stake because I'm bound and determined to keep it."

But as much as Hadley wished she could buy into that, she couldn't.

"Don't count me out because of my history with women, Hadley. I've rolled with all the changes in my friendship with Logan—that's part of what told me I could roll with any changes with you, too. If I can be friends with the same person for the biggest part of my life, with no end in sight, I can be married the same way."

"It's a whole lot easier to be a friend than a husband," Hadley said sadly. "And I don't want to be—I won't be—the one woman who ends up proving to you that you were right about marriage not being for you."

"Then at least stay—live with me or whatever until I can convince you that we belong together long-term—"

"That would do the same damage when it ended," she said, standing her ground.

"No damage is going to get done because there isn't going to be an end!" he said, raising his voice.

Then, just when the air was thick with emotion, when there was no denying that something heated was passing between them, Logan came into the workshop.

"What's going on?" he asked with a confused, troubled frown.

Hadley's mind spun.

Should she say Chase was unhappy with her decision to leave them hanging for an upholsterer?

Should she say they'd just had a disagreement or a difference of opinion over some work?

But before she could choose one, she saw Chase look Logan straight in the eye and heard him say, "I'll tell you what's going on—I'm crazy in love with your sister."

Chapter Twelve

"Maybe I ought to talk to her alone…"

Hadley heard her brother say that to Chase but she couldn't see anything—after Chase's announcement to Logan that he was crazy in love with her, she'd dropped her gaze to the cutting table she was standing behind, wondering how she'd gotten herself into this situation.

"All right," Chase agreed, "but I want her to marry me, Logan, and she's mixing me up with that jerk who cheated on her—she doesn't think I can be faithful or go the distance. Don't let her out of here until you've sold her on me."

"Let us talk, huh?" was Logan's only answer.

There was a long moment of silence when she wasn't sure if Chase and her brother were staring each other down. She also wasn't sure she wanted to know, so she didn't peek.

Then, her brother came to her side, hooked his arm under hers and urged her to raise her head. "Come on, Had, let's go to your place."

Hadley stood straight just in time to see the back of Chase as he headed for the stairs to the loft. That parting sight of him was enough to wrench her heart.

He wants me to marry him...

If only things were different...

But they weren't. And she had to be strong, she told herself. She had to be.

"Come on," her brother repeated, leading her to the workshop door.

Outside, in the cold October air, she knew she had to do some damage control. So as she and Logan walked to her garage apartment, she said, "It isn't what you're thinking. This doesn't have anything to do with the crush I had on Chase when we were kids. Well, maybe the old crush provided some of the underpinnings, but that honestly isn't where this all came from. And Chase still doesn't even know I ever had a crush on him."

"I knew something was going on with the two of you the minute we got back from our honeymoon—you've both been so...I don't know...so polite to each other. But I thought maybe you'd had a fight or something."

"There was definitely no fighting," Hadley muttered more to herself than to her brother as she let them both into her apartment. "But don't worry, I'm not stupid enough to believe anything could work out with Chase," she said to ease her brother's mind. "He's just not taking it too well. He's probably not all that accustomed to any woman turning him down for anything."

Logan didn't comment on that. He closed the apartment door behind them, and went to perch on the arm of her sofa, merely watching her as she began to pace the living room.

"Tell me what this is all about," he said.

After Chase's announcement it seemed silly to downplay anything, so Hadley was candid with her brother, including the details of what had just happened in the workshop and how she'd answered Chase's proposal.

"Of course I'm not the one woman who could change his mind about marriage!" she said when she'd finished with the details of the events that had led them to this point. "If ever there was a confirmed bachelor, it's Chase—it was like an early childhood imprint on him that marriage makes people miserable. I don't know that any woman could erase that but I know I can't—"

"Why not?" Logan asked, scowling at her.

She stopped pacing to look at her brother, wondering if she was misinterpreting his reaction. "Why not?" she parroted his words.

"I always thought that Chase would eventually meet somebody who would change what he thought about getting married. Why couldn't it be you?"

Hadley was dumbfounded for the second time tonight. Did her brother actually not hate the idea of her being with his best friend?

"Because...I'm just me, Logan!" she said in a voice raised with frustration.

"You're just who he says he loves."

"So you are trying to sell me on him?" she marveled.

He shrugged. "I know how you've felt about Chase since you were a kid, remember? And now he says he's crazy in love with you. He's never—ever—said that about anybody else, Hadley. Maybe you're the one person who can make him believe in marriage."

No wonder they're friends, they think alike...

"Look," Logan said then, "you're right when it comes to my friendship with Chase and to the business. It would be a mess if you two couldn't make it work out between you. But I think you're getting in your own way here, Had. I think that you have a lot of baggage that's making you believe that you couldn't be the one woman for him. And that's just wrong. You're beautiful, you're nice, you're fun, you're great—"

"Sometimes you two even sound alike," Hadley said, shirking off her brother's compliments to make him stop.

"I also think that you're reading Chase wrong— yes, he's done a lot of playing around when it comes to women. But I can tell you that he's never cheated. And he's never, ever, made a promise to any woman—to anyone—that he's broken—"

"He just doesn't make promises—isn't that what the lawsuit he won proved? No breach of promise because he didn't promise anything?"

"To Courtney. And no, he isn't free with his promises to women, but whenever he's made one, he's kept it. The point is, he's never led any woman on. He doesn't lie to them, he doesn't—"

"He told me that. That women had even testified to it—that's what won him his lawsuit."

"And now he's here promising you the moon, begging you to marry him. That means a lot, Had. A lot."

"It's just because of you. It's the only way he figures he can—"

"Not a chance," Logan said, shaking his head.

Logan paused a moment before he said, "Of course, none of this means squat if you don't have feelings for Chase…"

Why did she have to fight not to cry all of sudden?

That was crazy.

But it was true.

"Do you have feelings for Chase?" Logan asked quietly.

Hadley closed her eyes and swallowed back the tears so they didn't fall.

"Can you say you're crazy in love with him, too?" her brother persisted.

But her brother apparently didn't need to hear her answer to guess the truth, because when she'd successfully conquered the tears, she opened her eyes to find him shaking his head again, his expression sympathetic.

"That's the crux of the matter right there," he said. "Your feelings for him. His feelings for you. That's why I can't be the reason you say no to him. You're denying yourself and him something that I think you both want." Logan stood from his perch on the arm of the sofa. "But I'll tell you something else," he added.

Hadley raised her chin in question.

"I trust Chase. I trust you. And I'm not willing to be what keeps the two of you apart. So that can't—it cannot—carry any weight in what makes you choose one way or another. I want your promise on that."

Hadley only answered him with a raise of her eyebrows, unsure how wise that demand was.

Then Logan crossed to her and gave her a hug.

"I have faith in both of you, and I vote that you throw the dice, Had," her brother said before he left her alone with her own thoughts.

Hadley watched her brother close her apartment door behind him, then went to the raised platform that was the bedroom section of her studio apartment.

She kicked off her shoes, stepped onto the mattress of the sleigh bed and looked out the window.

Although the former barn that housed Chase's loft was next door to her garage apartment, the barn stretched farther back than the garage did. Early in the course of the week she'd spent helping Chase with Cody, she'd learned that if she craned over the headboard and looked out the window above her bed, she could see into the loft. And tonight she was using that tactic to see if—when her brother left her—he went to talk to Chase.

He did.

Neither of them looked happy, but they didn't seem to be arguing or exchanging any kind of heated words. They just talked, and if anything, she had the impression that Logan was offering Chase a message similar to what he'd given her—peppered with several shrugs that made it look as if Logan wasn't being very reassuring.

Logan spent about the same amount of time with Chase, too, before he was gone and she was watching Chase alone again.

His window was a big one that went from floor to ceiling and she could see that he was standing behind his couch. He was leaning on outstretched arms, his hands on the sofa back, his head hanging lower than his shoulders.

He looked angry and unhappy and all-round miserable, and that wrenched her heart even more than when she'd watched him leave the workshop.

But he thought marriage was what he wanted now?

That was just such a giant leap...

At least it was for her. It hadn't seemed that way for Chase. Or even for Logan.

What if she let herself buy what her brother had been selling—that Chase was loyal to a fault, that he kept promises, that he wasn't commitment-phobic, that he was merely conservative with the commitments he made because he did keep them?

She wanted to believe all of that and the more she thought about it, the more she realized that she didn't have any reason not to.

There was no disputing the level of commitment and loyalty that Chase showed Logan, the level of commitment he had to their business.

And Chase had been loyal to her, too, she realized.

When they were kids, he'd stood up for her. Defended her. Championed her. There was loyalty in that. And honor and strength and kindness and consideration. Maybe the sort of loyalty, of kindness, of care and consideration for her feelings that would keep him from ever hurting her the way her ex-husband's cheating had.

So was Chase offering her a commitment he would keep?

It was harder and harder for her not to waver.

When she honestly thought about it, she couldn't question that something deep and powerful had developed between them. Chase had opened up to her—she knew that he'd been every bit as invested as she had been, every bit as carried away. Nothing was one-sided—the way it had been when she'd had that crush on him. And if nothing was one-sided now, there was no more of a chance that that would change for him than that it would change for her, was there?

Hadley rested her head against the cold glass of the

window, still staring at Chase through her contorted view.

The man was so wonderful to look at. Even dressed unspectacularly in simple, worn jeans and a plain beige-colored polo shirt, he was something she didn't want to take her eyes off of.

Maybe Cody stirred just then, because Chase raised his head from its slump and, after a glance over his shoulder, pushed off the sofa and headed in the direction of the baby's room.

Cody. There was still Cody, Hadley reminded herself.

Chase had decided to keep him. To raise him. That showed loyalty and commitment, too.

As she went on watching the window in the loft, Chase came back into the living-room area. He didn't have Cody with him.

Rather than returning to his stance behind the couch, Chase went to the window.

He didn't look out, though. Instead he took a stance similar to the one he'd been in behind the couch—his arms were outstretched, his hands were splayed high up on the glass, and he dropped his head downward as if he were studying the one knee bent slightly forward in front of the other.

And Hadley wanted him so much it actually hurt.

That's the big one right there—your feelings for him, his feelings for you...

Logan's words echoed in her mind as everything

she'd been fighting suddenly swept through her with such force it nearly doubled her over.

She might have refused to confide her feelings for Chase to her brother because she'd thought that once she admitted to them, there would be no going back, but now she knew there was no going back anyway.

Not when what she felt for Chase was so clearly, so hugely, so potently not that simple crush of long ago.

Throw the dice, Had...

Those were her brother's parting words to her.

Logan had faith in her.

Logan had faith in Chase.

Logan was willing to gamble on them.

And if she gambled on them, too?

There was no doubt that it could be catastrophic if it didn't work out.

But what if it did?

Then it could be a long-ago dream come true.

Marrying Chase Mackey...

There was so much at stake...

But suddenly she just didn't know how she could do anything else.

Chapter Thirteen

"I'm sorry, but it has to be a few more minutes." Hadley apologized to Chase even though she was doing it from the window above the bed in her apartment while he was across the yard, leaning maudlinly against his own living-room window, with no idea that she'd just come to the decision to accept his marriage proposal.

But as a safety precaution to keep herself from giving in to temptation and getting anywhere near him during the past three weeks, she'd shaved her legs infrequently. And there was no way she could run to him now—the way she wanted to—without doing it.

So she bounded across the bed and ran to the shower.

Showering, shaving, shampooing—she spent the

whole time reassuring herself she was doing the right thing, that everything would be fine, hoping and praying that it would be, even as she tried to let it sink in that she was actually about to do what she was about to do.

After the shower she rushed through applying a little blush, a little mascara, a little lipgloss and doing her hair so it fell in a smooth, shiny curtain to dip just under her chin.

She put more care into choosing her underwear—a black lace thong and matching demi-cup bra—than in picking out the fanny-hugging jeans and cardigan sweater she wore over them. Then it took equally as long to decide how many of the sweater's buttons to button and how many to leave undone.

She wasn't trying to seduce Chase, she reminded herself. She was going to make up with him, to make amends, to say yes to his proposal.

She ended up buttoning only the middle three of the sweater's buttons—leaving the bottom two open to expose her belly button where it showed over the waistband of her low-riding jeans, and the top four unfastened to expose some cleavage, too.

A dash of the excessively expensive French perfume she saved for the most special occasions, and she was out the door.

She was hit by a sudden case of nerves as she went down the stairs alongside the garage, but then she saw her brother watching from the window above the kitchen sink in the main house.

Apparently she'd left little question about what she was going to do, because Logan grinned from ear to ear and gave her a thumbs-up that—for no reason she could explain—made tears well in her eyes.

But she didn't want to be crying when she saw Chase, so she blinked back the tears as she waved to her brother and headed for the loft.

Knowing that Logan was watching, it was tempting to go into the workroom first and enter unannounced by the stairs that led from there to Chase's place. But somehow that seemed presumptuous. She didn't believe that Chase could reverse his thinking in the short time since he'd come down to the workroom to talk to her, but she was afraid to assume anything.

So, knowing she was under the watchful eye of her brother, she used the outside steps that rose to Chase's deck, crossed it and knocked on his door.

Chase's "come in" was muffled, and Hadley felt sure that he thought she was Logan. But she went in anyway, finding Chase's back to her where he stood across the loft with his cell phone at his ear, talking to someone.

Her own stress level mounted but she merely stood with her back to the door, waiting for Chase to turn around and see that she was there.

"No, I'm just glad you called," she heard him say into the phone in the meantime. "Believe me, I know what a shock it is to find out you have family—well, I guess biological family is the term, you have adopted family that's probably who you consider family…"

Was he talking to his sister?

Hadley knew he'd called Shannon Duffy several times without reaching her, that he'd recently resorted to writing her a letter to introduce himself. Had his long-lost sister finally gotten in touch with him? And if she had, Hadley wasn't sure she should be there listening in. Or doing what she'd come to do right now.

Maybe I should just slip back out...

But about the time that thought ran through her mind, Chase turned around.

"Oh! Wow!" he said, obviously surprised to see her.

Then, after what appeared to be a moment of disorientation, he said into the phone, "No, Shannon, I wasn't talking to you. I'm sorry, something has just come up. I don't mean to cut you off but could I call you tomorrow and talk more?"

There was a pause while Chase stood there, his sky-blue eyes boring into Hadley, his brows furrowed as he stared at her a bit dumbfoundedly and obviously only half listened to whatever the answer on the other end of the line was.

Then, again into the phone, he said, "Thanks. I really appreciate it. I'll talk to you in the morning."

He took the cell phone down from his ear, closing it without ever taking his eyes off Hadley, without seeming to have any awareness of what he was doing. Of anything but her.

"Shannon? As in Shannon Duffy—your sister?" Hadley asked.

He nodded. "She spent the last month in Europe and her phone didn't work over there. She just got back and heard all my messages, got the letter I wrote her last week…"

Chase was answering the question Hadley had asked but that was clearly not his primary concern.

Then he said, "When I heard the knock on the door I thought it was—"

"Logan," Hadley finished for him. "I figured."

His frown grew more perplexed as his gaze dropped to the open invitation of her sweater. When he looked at her face again, he said, "You turned me down to go home and change clothes?"

Hadley shook her head. "I turned you down for all the reasons I told you I was turning you down. Then I talked to Logan and thought about some things—"

"I know you talked to Logan—he came here afterward. But he didn't give me much hope." Chase paused, then said, "I'm a little raw here, Had. Don't mess with me."

There was a look in his eyes—a vulnerability—that she'd never seen before and she hated that she'd put it there.

"I didn't come to mess with you," she said quietly. Then, in a feeble attempt to ease some of the tension in the air, she joked, "Well, not in a bad way."

"You came to mess with me in a good way before

you leave town?" he asked, sounding as raw as he said he was.

She shook her head. "I told you—I talked to Logan and I thought about some things—"

"Logan gave us the go-ahead. He—"

"I know. It still weighs on me that there's so much on the line with the two of you, but it helps that Logan wants that not to be a factor. That he isn't against us being together."

"And the rest?"

"There was a lot that Logan said about who you are— deep down…things I know are true, that I didn't think about…" Hadley shrugged, struggling to find the words. "I know you're a good guy," she finally said. "But I also know you've been around—a lot—and you said yourself that marriage was not for you. It was just hard to believe you could switch gears so fast and I don't want to be Alma Pritick—married to somebody who liked me at the start but doesn't even want to talk to me down the line…"

"I don't just like you…"

"Still, there's that bloom-wearing-off thing, that getting annoyed and—"

Chase smiled slightly, kindly, compassionately at her. "What we have together is worth a little tussle every now and then to keep it going. It's worth anything to me to keep it going. So tell me that's why you're here—that with Logan's blessing and some more thinking you want that damn *no* back so you can replace it with a yes…"

That made her smile slightly, too. "I do want my no back," she whispered. "If you still—"

"Oh, I still," he confirmed, crossing to her as if he'd just broken through the ribbon at the finish line.

When he reached her he took her upper arms in his big hands, looked deeply into her eyes and said hopefully, "You'll marry me?"

"I will. If you're sure. If you really, really believe—"

"I believe," he said, holding tight to her arms. "I believe in you and me. I believe I never had any damn idea what love honestly was or felt like until now, and now I believe that it can move mountains and part seas and definitely, definitely make marriages work. I believe that love and marriage and lasting forever can work for us if you'll just let me prove it to you."

"Well, here I am," Hadley said.

"Because you believe, too, right?"

Hadley answered him with certainty. "I do. I believe in you and me, too."

"Because you know I love you," Chase said quietly, sincerely.

And as Hadley looked up into that handsome face, she did know, instinctively, through and through, that he loved her.

So all she said was, "I love you, too, Chase."

A myriad of emotions crossed his features then, from relief to happiness to something that resembled a very appealing cockiness before he pulled her to him and gave her a kiss that went through some stages, too—starting out warm and soft and tender before the heat turned up and three weeks' worth of hunger and yearning and frustration came into play.

Chase wrapped his arms around her then, holding her tight against him as his mouth opened wide over hers and their kiss deepened.

Her arms snaked under his so she could press her hands to his broad back, and in that moment she knew she would never have been able to go the rest of her life without this, without this man.

Urgency and an all-consuming need swept them away then. Clothes flew off and willing bodies met, skin to skin.

The bedroom was too far away and they ended up stretched out on that leather couch Chase had been leaning against earlier.

"The window..." Hadley moaned as his mouth worked magic at her breast and a glance down at his head there reminded her of that view she'd had of him before. "You can see into it from the apartment..."

Chase leaned over her to grab a remote control off of the coffee table. He pushed a button and the blinds slid closed.

"Better?" he asked in a passion-ravaged voice.

"As long as my brother doesn't come barging in the door to see what's going on..."

Chase grinned. "Logan's not that dumb," he assured

as he recaptured her mouth with his and reignited the flames between them all over again.

And even if Hadley had wanted to think of anything else from then on, she couldn't. Not with Chase wiping away all awareness of anything but him and what he was doing to her, what he was arousing in her.

Arousing in her and then cultivating, feeding, making it flourish until he was where she'd wanted him to be ever since they'd parted three weeks before—holding her, inside of her, climbing with her to make explosive love that forged more than a physical bond between them, that entwined them heart and soul, and brought home that what they had with each other was too profound to be left by the wayside.

"I love you more than you will ever know, Hadley," Chase whispered gruffly when ecstasy had been found and released, when they'd caught their breath, when they were lying together depleted and drained, with every need met, warm naked flesh pressed to warm naked flesh.

Hadley craned her head back to look up at him. "I loved you more than you did know," she said with a small smile.

Chase scowled down at her. "What does that mean?"

"When we were kids—I had the biggest crush on you…"

"You did?" he said as if he couldn't believe it.

"The biggest," she repeated.

"I didn't know…"

"You weren't supposed to."

"It's okay, though," he said, his arms tightening around her as if he liked the thought. "Because now I have the biggest crush on you."

"You better have more than a crush on me," she chastised playfully.

"Oh, I do." He rolled to his side so he could face her then, kissed the top of her head and said, "I'm thinking maybe a Christmas wedding—what do you say to that?"

"Two months?"

"Nothing too rushed, but I can't wait for long."

"Two months to plan a wedding is a rush," Hadley informed him.

"We can do it, though, don't you think? I mean it—I can't wait longer than that."

"Maybe your sister will come…"

"I don't know, it took me a month just to get her to call back. But maybe. And that'd be kind of nice, wouldn't it? Then I'd have family there, too."

"It would be nice," Hadley agreed, thinking that this was the first time he'd mentioned his newfound family with any sort of pleasure.

"And Cody?" Chase said then. "We can't forget him—you know it isn't just that I want help raising him, don't you?"

"I do. I'm sorry for that jab before. You've been doing a great job with him without me."

"But I want to do it with you."

Hadley smiled at him again. "I think that's what I just signed on for tonight, isn't it?"

"I guess we have become a package deal—Cody and me—haven't we?"

"And who knows?" Hadley said, "By Christmas you could even know where your brothers are and invite them, too. Between Cody and your lost sister and brothers and whatever spouses or kids or other brothers and sisters they might have, you could end up with more family than you know what to do with."

"The Mackeys and the McKendricks—we'll make it an empire," he joked. "But at the end of every day, it still needs to be just you and me—promise me that."

"Just you and me," Hadley confirmed, knowing that what had brought them together, what held them together, what would go on holding them together was simply what was between the two of them.

Chase kissed her again with a new poignancy, then dropped his head to the sofa seat and said in a weary voice, "Logan's gonna want to know how we did—"

Hadley laughed. "Excuse me?" she said, knowing what Chase meant but using the way it sounded to tease him.

Chase grinned with his eyes closed. "He'll want to know that we worked everything out," he amended. "But let's give it a few minutes, huh? Then we'll tell him."

"Okay," Hadley agreed, in no hurry to leave the comfort and solace of Chase's arms.

And as she settled in for a short rest herself, she thought fleetingly of that lonely boy Chase had been long ago who had come to her rescue, who had filled her fantasies, and she suddenly knew without question that it wasn't catastrophe that would come of this.

That this genuinely was a dream come true.

And that together they had only the best to look forward to from that moment on.

* * * * *

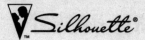

COMING NEXT MONTH

Available August 31, 2010

REQUEST YOUR FREE BOOKS!

2 FREE NOVELS PLUS 2 FREE GIFTS!

SPECIAL EDITION
Life, Love and Family!

HARLEQUIN®

A Romance

FOR EVERY MOOD™

Spotlight on

Heart & Home

Heartwarming romances
where love can happen
right when you least expect it.

See the next page to enjoy a sneak peek
from Harlequin Superromance®,
a Heart and Home series.

Police chief Juliette Tremblant recognized the shape of the man strolling down the street—in as calm and leisurely fashion as if it were the middle of the day rather than midnight. She slowed her car, convinced her eyes were playing tricks on her. It had been a long time since Tyler O'Neill had been seen in this town.

As she pulled to a stop at the curb, he turned toward her, and her heart about stopped.

"What the hell are you doing here, Tyler?"

"Well, if it isn't Juliette Tremblant." He made his way over to her, then leaned down so he could look her in the eye. He was close enough to touch.

Juliette was not, repeat, *not* going to touch Tyler O'Neill. Not with her fingers. Not with a ten-foot pole. There would be no touching. Which was too bad, since it was the only way she was ever going to convince herself the man standing in front of her—as rumpled and heart-stoppingly handsome now as he'd been at sixteen—was real.

And not a figment of all her furious revenge dreams.

"What are you doing back in Bonne Terre?" she asked.

"The manor is sitting empty," Tyler said and shrugged, as though his arriving out of the blue after ten years was casual. "Seems like someone should be watching over the family home."

"You?" She laughed at the very notion of him being here for any unselfish reason. "Please."

He stared at her for a second, then smiled. Her heart fluttered against her chest—a small mechanical bird powered by that smile.

"You're right." But that cryptic comment was all he offered.

Juliette bit her lip against the other questions.

Why did you go?

Why didn't you write? Call?

What did I do?

But what would be the point? Ten years of silence were all the answer she really needed.

She had sworn off feeling anything for this man long ago. Yet one look at him and all the old hurt and rage resurfaced as though they'd been waiting for the chance. That made her mad.

She put the car in gear, determined not to waste another minute thinking about Tyler O'Neill. "Have a good night, Tyler," she said, liking all the cool "go screw yourself" she managed to fit into those words.

It seems Juliette has an old score to settle with Tyler.
Pick up TYLER O'NEILL'S REDEMPTION
to see how he makes it up to her.
Available September 2010,
only from Harlequin Superromance.

MARGARET WAY

introduces

THE
Rylance
DYNASTY

**The lives & loves of
Australia's most powerful family**

Growing up in the spotlight hasn't been easy, but the two
Rylance heirs, Corin and his sister, Zara, have come of age
and are ready to claim their inheritance. Though they are
privileged, proud and powerful, they are about to discover
that there are some things money can't buy....

Look for:

Australia's Most Eligible Bachelor
Available September

Cattle Baron Needs a Bride
Available October